THE
PROFESSIONAL

THE PROFESSIONAL

Robert B. Parker

Doubleday Large Print Home Library Edition

G. P. PUTNAM'S SONS

New York

This Large Print Edition, prepared especially for Double-day Large Print Home Library, contains the complete, unabridged text of the original Publisher's Edition.

PUTNAM

G. P. PUTNAM'S SONS
Publishers Since 1838
Published by the Penguin Group
Penguin Group (USA) Inc., 375 Hudson Street, New York, New York 10014, USA • Penguin Group (Canada), 90 Eglinton Avenue East, Suite 700, Toronto, Ontario M4P 2Y3, Canada (a division of Pearson Canada Inc.) • Penguin Books Ltd, 80 Strand, London WC2R 0RL, England • Penguin Ireland, 25 St Stephen's Green, Dublin 2, Ireland (a division of Penguin Books Ltd) • Penguin Group (Australia), 250 Camberwell Road, Camberwell, Victoria 3124, Australia (a division of Pearson Australia Group Pty Ltd) • Penguin Books India Pvt Ltd, 11 Community Centre, Panchsheel Park, New Delhi–110 017, India • Penguin Group (NZ), 67 Apollo Drive, Rosedale, North Shore 0632, New Zealand (a division of Pearson New Zealand Ltd) • Penguin

Books (South Africa) (Pty) Ltd, 24 Sturdee Avenue,
Rosebank, Johannesburg 2196, South Africa

Penguin Books Ltd, Registered Offices:
80 Strand, London WC2R 0RL, England

ISBN-13: 978-1-61523-536-0

Printed in the United States of America

BOOK DESIGN BY AMANDA DEWEY

This is a work of fiction. Names, characters, places,
and incidents either are the product of the author's
imagination or are used fictitiously, and any resemblance

to actual persons, living or dead, businesses, companies, events, or locales is entirely coincidental.

While the author has made every effort to provide accurate telephone numbers and Internet addresses at the time of publication, neither the publisher nor the author assumes any responsibility for errors, or for changes that occur after publication. Further, the publisher does not have any control over and does not assume any responsibility for author or third-party websites or their content.

This Large Print Book carries the
Seal of Approval of N.A.V.H.

For Emma, who arrived; and
for Gracie, who left.

THE
PROFESSIONAL

Chapter

❖❖

1

I HAD JUST FINISHED a job for an interesting woman named Nan Sartin, and was happily making out my bill to her, when a woman came in who promised to be equally interesting.

It was a bright October morning when she walked into my office carrying a briefcase. She was a big woman, not fat, but strong-looking and very graceful. Her hair was silver, and her face was young enough to make me assume that the silver was premature. She was wearing a dark blue suit with a long jacket and a short skirt.

I said, "Hello."

She said, "My name is Elizabeth Shaw. Please call me Elizabeth. I'm an attorney, and I represent a group of women who need your help."

She took a business card from her briefcase and placed it on my desk. It said she was a partner in the law firm Shaw and Cartwright, and that they had offices on Milk Street.

I said, "Okay."

"You are Spenser," she said.

"I am he," I said.

"I specialize in wills and trusts," she said. "I know little about criminal law."

I nodded.

"But I went to law school with Rita Fiore," she said.

So the silver hair was premature.

"Ahh," I said.

She smiled.

"Ahh, indeed," she said. "So I told Rita my story, and she suggested I tell it to you."

"Please do," I said.

Elizabeth Shaw looked at the large picture of Susan that sat on my file drawer near the coffeemaker.

"Is that your wife?" she said.

"Sort of," I said.

"How can she be 'sort of'?" Elizabeth said.

"We're not married," I said.

"But?"

"But we've been together a considerable time," I said.

"And you love her," Elizabeth said.

"I do."

"And she loves you."

"She does."

"Then why don't you get married?" Elizabeth said.

"I don't know," I said.

She stared at me. I smiled pleasantly. She frowned a little.

"Was there anything else?" I said.

She smiled suddenly. It was a good look for her.

"I'm sorry," she said. "I guess I was trying to find out a little about your attitude toward women and marriage."

"I try to develop my attitudes on a case-by-case basis," I said.

She nodded, thinking about it.

"Rita says there's no one better if the going gets rough."

"Uh-huh."

"How about if the going isn't rough?" Elizabeth said.

"There's still no one better," I said.

"Rita mentioned that you didn't lack for confidence."

"Would you want someone who did?" I said.

I must have passed some kind of initial screening. She shifted in her chair slightly.

"Everything I tell you," she said, "must, of course, remain entirely confidential."

"Sure."

She looked at Susan's picture again.

"That's a very beautiful woman," she said.

"She is," I said.

She shifted again in her chair.

"I have a client, a woman, married, with a substantial trust fund, given to her by her husband as a wedding present. We manage the trust for her, and over the years she and I have become friendly."

"He gave her a trust fund for a present?" Elizabeth smiled.

"The rich are very different," she said.

"Yes," I said. "They have more money."

"Well," she said. "A literate detective."

"But self-effacing."

She smiled again.

"My client's name is Abigail Larson," Elizabeth said. "She is considerably younger than her husband."

"How considerably?"

"He's sixty-eight. She's thirty-one."

"Aha," I said.

"'Aha'?"

"I'm jumping to a conclusion," I said.

"Sadly, the conclusion is correct. She had an affair."

"Lot of that going around," I said.

"You disapprove?" Elizabeth said.

"I guess it's probably better if people can be faithful to each other," I said.

"She's not a bad woman," Elizabeth said.

"Affairs aren't usually about good and bad," I said.

"What do you think they're about?"

"Need," I said.

Elizabeth sat back a little in her chair.

"You're not what I expected," she said.

"Hell," I said. "I'm not what I expected. What would you like me to do?"

"I'm sorry. I guess I'm still testing you."

"Maybe you could test my ability to listen to what you want," I said.

She smiled at me.

"Yes," she said. "In brief, the man she had the affair with took her for some money and ditched her."

"How much?" I said.

"Actually, just enough to hurt her feelings. Restaurants, hotels, car rentals, a small gift now and then."

"And?" I said.

"That was it," Elizabeth said, "for a while. Then one day she saw him, in a restaurant, with a woman whom she knew casually."

"Nest prospecting," I said.

"Apparently," Elizabeth said. "Anyway, she talked to the woman the next day to tell her a little about her experience with this guy. . . ."

"Whose name is?" I said.

"Gary Eisenhower," Elizabeth said.

"Gary Eisenhower?" I said.

Elizabeth shrugged.

"That's what he tells them," she said.

"Them?"

"The two women talked, and then they networked, and one thing led to another, and in ways too boring to detail here, they discovered that he had exploited four of them, often simultaneously, over the past ten years."

"Have you met this guy?"

"No."

"Well, if you do," I said, "be careful."

"I think I'll be all right," she said.

"So the seduced and abandoned have joined forces?" I said.

"Yes."

"And what do they want?"

"They'd like to see him castrated, I'm sure, but that's not why I'm here."

"Oh, good," I said.

"They came to me as a group because I was the only lawyer that any of them knew, and we agreed that pursuing him for the money would cause them embarrassment. Their husbands would find out. It might make a great tabloid story. So they agreed to move on, sadder but wiser, so to speak."

"But," I said.

"But he has returned. He has contacted each of them. He says he has proof positive of each adultery and will expose them to their husbands and the world if they don't pay him."

"What kind of evidence?" I said.

"They thought they were being discreet," Elizabeth said. "These women are not stupid, nor, I guess, inexperienced."

"No letters," I said. "No e-mails, no messages on answering machines."

"Yes."

"Hidden cameras, hidden tape recorders?"

Elizabeth nodded.

"Uh-huh," she said. "I guess he was planning on shaking them down all along."

"Maybe," I said. "Sometimes people like to keep a record. Allows them to revisit these special moments, when things are slow."

"So," Elizabeth said, "maybe shaking them down was an afterthought?"

"Maybe," I said. "They don't want to pay."

"Don't want to, and can't. Their husbands control all of the substantial money."

"So you want me to make him cease and desist, without causing a stir," I said.

"Can you?" she said.

"Sure," I said.

Chapter

✦

2

I MET THE FOUR WOMEN in a bigger conference room than we needed at Shaw and Cartwright. Elizabeth Shaw sat at one side of the table. The women sat two apiece on each side of her. I sat across from them.

Elizabeth introduced them.

"Abigail Larson, Beth Jackson, Regina Hartley, Nancy Sinclair."

They each had a small notepad in front of them. And a ballpoint pen. Doubtless provided by the firm. They all smiled at me. All of the smiles displayed white, even teeth. They were all extremely well dressed. They all had very good haircuts. They all looked in shape. None looked older than thirty-five. It is easier to be good-looking when you're thirty-five, and even easier if you're rich. Though Elizabeth Shaw, who was probably neither, was holding her own. I smiled back at all of them.

No one said anything. They all looked at Elizabeth.

"Perhaps you could tell us a little about yourself," Elizabeth said to me.

"I used to be a cop, now I'm a private detective," I said.

"Do you have a gun?" Regina said.

"I do."

"Have you ever shot anyone?" she said.

"I have."

"Could you tell us about that?" she said.

"No."

"Well, for heaven's sake," Regina said.

She had very black hair, which she wore in bangs over her forehead. Her eyes were large and made to seem larger by her eye makeup. She had on a simple print dress that had probably cost more than Liechtenstein, and her skin was evenly tanned, which in October, in Boston, meant she had either traveled to warmer climes or used an excellent bronzer.

"If we're going to hire you, I think we should be able to ask you questions," Abigail said.

I think she was trying to sound stern, but her voice was too small for stern.

"You can ask anything you want," I said. "Doesn't mean I have to answer."

"Well, how are we supposed to decide," she said.

"Me telling you about shooting somebody won't help."

Abigail was blonde, with a short haircut that had probably cost as much as Regina's little dress. Her eyes were blue. She looked tan.

"I just think it would be so interesting," she said. "I mean, I bet nobody here even knows anyone who has shot someone."

"I am hopeful that I won't have to shoot anyone on this job," I said.

Abigail said, "I wouldn't actually mind if you shot the bastard."

"No," Beth said. "I don't think any of us would mind."

Both Beth and Abigail were blonde. In fact, everyone at the table was blonde except Regina, and me, and Elizabeth. Maybe they did have more fun.

"Tell me about him," I said.

All the women looked at Abigail. She shrugged.

"He's one slick item," she said. "He's handsome, charming, fun to be with, wears clothes beautifully, and he's very sexy, the sonovabitch."

"So far, except for sonovabitch," I said, "we could be talking about me."

The women all looked at me without response.

"So much for lighthearted," I said. "Can you give me anything more substantive? Like where he lives?"

"I . . ." Abigail paused. "I don't actually know."

"Who does," I said.

They all looked at one another and discovered that none of them knew. It startled them.

"Okay," I said. "Where did you get together?"

"We'd meet for cocktails," Abigail said. "Or drinks and dinner in, like, suburban restaurants. At least that's what he and I did."

All the other women nodded. That's what they did, too.

"And where did you, ah, consummate your relationship," I said.

Spenser, the soul of delicacy.

"I, for one, am not going to discuss that," Regina said.

"Oh, for crissake, Reggie," Abigail said. "How the hell did he get the goods on you?"

She looked at me.

"We were all bopping our brains out with him," she said. "With me it was usually in a motel along 128."

"Sometimes we'd go away for a weekend," Beth said. "Maine, the Cape, New York City."

Beth had a small, attractive overbite, and wore sunglasses that probably cost more than Abigail's haircut.

"Did you go often to the same motels?" I said.

"I did," Abigail said. "There was one near the Burlington Mall we went to four, five times."

"The one with the little fountain in the lobby?" Regina said.

All of them had been there. He had several favorites that all of them had been to. They showed no geographic pattern.

"And no one has an address for him," I said.

No one did.

"Or a phone number?"

They had phone numbers, but they weren't the same numbers.

"I'll make a prediction," I said. "These will all turn out to be prepaid disposable cell phones."

"Which means?" Elizabeth said.

"That we won't know who the owner was or where he lived."

"It sounds as if he didn't ever want us to be able to find him," Regina said.

"Be my guess," I said.

"Then . . . that means . . . that means he was never, ever sincere, even at the start," she said.

This guy was really good, I thought. Even after he started blackmailing them, there was still the hope for something.

"Probably not," I said.

"So how can you ever find him?" Abigail said.

"It's not as hopeless as it sounds," I said. "Each of you has been with him, quite often. We'll talk, each of you and me. One of you, maybe more than one, will remember something."

"Do you really think you can find him?" Abigail said.

"Yes."

"How?"

"I'm very resourceful," I said.

"Can you be more specific?" Abigail said.

"No," I said.

"If you do find him," Regina said, "what will you do?"

I grinned at her.

"Step at a time," I said.

"But how will you make him leave us alone?" she said. "You look like you could beat him up. Will you beat him up?"

"Soon as I find him," I said.

Reggie seemed satisfied.

Chapter

3

SᴜꜱᴀN ᴀND I were having drinks before dinner in the South End at a slick new restaurant called Rocca. Susan was sipping a Cosmopolitan. I was moving more quickly on a Dewar's and soda.

"It's sort of an elaborate scam," Susan said. "Isn't it?"

"Kind of," I said. "But he gets a double dip out of it."

"Sex *and* money?" Susan said.

"Yep. With an assortment of handsome women."

"All of whom," Susan said, "are married to older men."

"Rich older men," I said.

"Doesn't mean none of them love their husbands," Susan said.

"No, it doesn't," I said. "But none of the women love their husbands enough to stay faithful."

"Often it's not a matter of love," Susan said.

"I know."

"Still," Susan said, "he chose wisely."

"Which suggests it's not random," I said.

My scotch was gone. I looked around for a waiter, and found one, and asked for more. A handsome, well-dressed man walked past our table with a group of people. The handsome man stopped.

"Susan," he said. "Hello."

"Joe," Susan said. "What a treat."

She introduced us.

"Joseph Abboud?" I said. "The clothes guy."

"The clothes guy," he said.

"You got anything off the rack would fit me?" I said.

Abboud looked at me silently for a moment and smiled.

"God, I hope not," he said.

We laughed. Abboud moved on after

his group. I drank my second scotch. We looked at the menu. The waitress took our order.

"Is that how you're going to find him?" Susan said. "That it's not random?"

"There must be some connection among the women and with him," I said.

"Do you have a thought?" Susan said. "On what it might be?"

"No," I said.

"But you will," she said.

"I will," I said.

"These women don't know each other?"

"They do now," I said. "But they didn't originally, except a couple of them."

"So what they have in common seems to be," Susan said, and smiled, "Gary Eisenhower."

"And rich older husbands," I said.

"And perhaps some evidence of promiscuity," Susan said. "I mean, every young wife doesn't cheat on her husband. Why did he think these women would?"

"Maybe they are the result of an exhaustive elimination process," I said.

"Despite what I've said, it may be optimistic to think it requires an exhaustive process," Susan said.

"So lovely, and yet so cynical," I said.

"My line of work," she said. "The success rate is not always startling."

"Hell," I said. "Neither is mine."

"I suppose, though," Susan said, "that we are both optimists in some sense. We believe that things can be made better."

"And sometimes we're right," I said.

"That's part of the payoff, isn't it," Susan said.

"Yes," I said. "Plus, of course, the fee."

Chapter

◆◆

4

ABIGAIL LARSON had seemed the most lively of my four clients. So I tried her first. She lived in Louisburg Square. But she wanted to meet at the bar at the Taj. Which was once the Ritz-Carlton. But the Ritz had opened a new location up on the other side of the Common, and the name moved up there.

Except for the unfortunate name, the Taj hadn't changed anything. So the bar was still good, and the view from a window table of the Public Garden across Arlington Street was still very good. It was ten to four in the afternoon, on a Thursday, and I had snared us a window table. Abigail was twenty minutes late, but I had been trained by Susan, who was always late except when it mattered. And I remained calm.

I stood when she came in. The bartender waved at her, and two waiters came to say hello as she came toward my table. She put out her hand. I shook it, one of the waiters held her chair, and she sat. She ordered a lemon-drop martini and smiled at me.

"You're drinking beer?"

"I am," I said.

"I get so full if I drink enough beer to get tipsy," she said. The smile continued. "A martini does the job on much less volume."

"I'm hoping not to get tipsy," I said.

"What fun is that?" she said.

Gary Eisenhower must have been delighted when he met her. She did everything but hand out business cards to let you know that she fooled around.

"Tell me about Gary," I said.

"I thought we already did that, in Shaw's office," she said.

Her lemon-drop martini arrived. She sampled it with pleasure.

"Smoothes out a day," she said.

I drank a little beer.

"I was hoping just sort of informally for some reminiscences," I said. "You know, how did you meet? Where did you go? What did you do?"

"What did we do?"

"Other than that," I said.

"You got something against 'that'?" she said.

"No," I said. "You can tell me about 'that,' too, if you like."

She smiled at me.

"Maybe I will," she said.

I waited.

"Actually," she said, and took in some more of her lemon drop, "I met him here."

She glanced around the room, looking for a waiter, spotted one, and nodded. He smiled and went to the bar.

"I come here quite often," she said.

"I suspected as much," I said.

"Often I go to my gym, in the late afternoon, and afterward I shower and change and meet my girlfriends for a cocktail."

"Replenish those electrolytes," I said.

"What?" she said.

I shook my head and smiled.

"Just musing out loud," I said.

"Anyway," she said. "I'd see him at the bar sometimes, and after two or three times, he'd smile and nod as I came in, and I'd do the same. One day I came in alone and sat at a table, and he was at the bar. I smiled at him and nodded, and he picked up his drink and walked over and asked if he could join me. . . . God, he was handsome."

She drank some more of her lemon drop. She took small, ladylike swallows. She didn't guzzle, but she was persistent.

"And he was very charming," I said.

"And sexy and fun," she said. "And we both had a couple of cocktails, and talked, and one thing led to another . . ."

"And," I said, "I'll bet he had a room in the hotel."

She looked at me for a moment as if I'd just performed necromancy.

"Yes," she said, "he did. And . . ." She shrugged.

"What's a girl to do," I said.

She nodded slowly, looking at the depleted surface of her lemon drop.

"I know now he was using me," she said. "But God, he was good."

She stopped staring into the martini and finished it.

"What gym do you go to?" I said.

"Pinnacle Fitness," she said.

"The big flossy thing on Tremont?" I said.

"You know it?" she said.

"I was there once with a client," I said.

Another lemon-drop martini arrived.

"Do you work out?"

"Some," I said.

"You look very fit," she said.

"You, too," I said.

Mistake.

She smiled again and her face flushed slightly.

"You should see me with my clothes off," she said.

"Probably should," I said.

She smiled again and her face flushed a little more.

"Do you have a room upstairs?" she said.

"Sadly, no," I said.

"I could probably get us one," she said.

"It's a kind offer," I said. "But no, thank you."

"Are you married?"

"No."

"But?"

"But I'm in love with Susan Silverman, and we've agreed on monogamy."

"My goodness," Abigail said.

"I know," I said. "Makes me kind of boring, but there it is."

"What a waste," she said.

"Everyone says that."

I drank another swallow of beer.

"When did the money stuff come up?" I said.

"Not right away. He paid for everything the first time we were together, here. I don't think he took any money from me for, oh, I'd say at least a year, year and a half. Then he said there was some waterfront property in Chatham, which was way underpriced, and he knew he could buy it, we could go there and spend time, and later when the market rose, he'd sell it for a nice profit."

"But all his money was tied up, and he didn't want to cash in a CD because of the penalties," I said. "So maybe you could lend him the down payment and you'd get it back with interest when the house was sold."

"That's almost exactly right," she said. "How did you know?"

"Amazing, isn't it?" I said. "You ever see the house?"

"Yes, we spent several weekends there."

"And your husband?"

"He thought I was with my girlfriends," Abigail said. "You know. He used to call it a sisterhood retreat."

"Your husband doesn't know," I said.

"God, no, that's the big reason we hired you."

"No suspicions? Then or now?"

"None. He's very busy and very important. Tell you the truth," she said, "I don't think it occurs to him that it could happen."

"You are intimate?"

"Sure. John's not in the very best shape, and he gets tired at night, and, you know, he's sixty-eight."

"So your intimacy is not as frequent as it might be," I said.

"Or as long-lasting, or as . . . ah, enthusiastic."

"So Gary Eisenhower was an appealing alternative."

"Very," she said. "I think I would have let him get away with the money."

"The ride was worth the money," I said.

"Yes. But the blackmail. I can't live that way, none of us can. My husband can't know."

"You have a picture of Gary?" I said.

"No, I threw them out as soon as I found out what he was," she said.

"Too bad."

"I didn't want my husband finding them, either."

"You love your husband?"

"Love?" She shrugged. "I care about him, certainly. Why do you ask?"

"Just a curious guy," I said.

Chapter

•◆•

5

IT WAS A LITTLE AFTER NINE in the morning on an overcast day with some thin fog in the air. I was drinking coffee and reading "Arlo & Janis" when Nancy Sinclair came carefully into my office, as if she was entering the confessional.

"Mr. Spenser?" she said. "I'm Nancy Sinclair, from the other day at Elizabeth Shaw's office?"

"Of course," I said.

As far as I could recall, she had not spoken when we had our meeting. She looked like a dressed-up cheerleader: a plaid skirt and a white shirt, dark stockings and boots.

She was small. Her hair was short and thick. Her jewelry was gold and simple, and so was her wedding band. Her eyes were blue and very big, and she seemed to have a look of permanent surprise, as if the world amazed her. She sat opposite me, in front of the desk, with her knees together and her hands folded in her lap. She didn't say anything.

"How 'bout them Sox?" I said.

She smiled brightly.

After a while I said, "How you doing?"

"Fine."

"Is there something you'd like to discuss?" I said.

She nodded.

"Is it about Gary Eisenhower?" I said.

She nodded again. I waited. She smiled at me hopefully. I nodded helpfully.

"I love my husband," she said.

"That's nice," I said.

"He loves me," she said.

"Also nice," I said.

"We love each other," she said.

"Good combo," I said.

"I don't . . ."

She seemed to be thinking of how to say whatever it was she wanted to say.

"I don't want you to get the wrong idea," she said.

"I'd be thrilled with any idea," I said.

She smiled brightly again. It was what she did when she didn't understand something. I was already pretty sure that understanding stuff wasn't a big part of her skill set.

"I did have an affair with Gary Eisenhower," she said. "I don't deny it. But it was not because Jim and I don't love each other."

"What was it because?" I said.

She blushed slowly but pervasively. It was kind of interesting watching the blush spread slowly over her face and down her neck, and onto the small expanse of chest that her white shirt collar exposed. She looked as if she might be blushing to her ankles.

"I'm oversexed," she said.

"Doesn't make you a bad person," I said.

"It does," she said. "I keep promising myself it will never happen again. But it does. I can't seem to stop myself."

"So Gary Eisenhower isn't the first," I said.

"God, no," she said. "I once had sex with

a man who came to plow the driveway. I'm . . . This is so embarrassing. . . . I'm insatiable."

"And your husband's not enough," I said.

"We have a good sex life. I'm just . . . I've fought it since junior high school. I am some sort of nymphomaniac."

I nodded.

"I think 'nymphomania' is sort of an unfashionable term these days," I said.

"Whatever," she said, her face still bright red under her makeup. "I'm addicted to sex. It is a shameful thing, and it has made my life very difficult."

"Ever talk to anyone about it?" I said.

"I talked once with the minister at our church, before I got married."

"And?"

"We prayed together," she said.

"At least he didn't ask you out," I said.

"Excuse me?"

I shook my head.

"My mouth sometimes operates independent of my brain," I said.

She smiled brightly.

"For a little while after we prayed together, it seemed almost as if it had worked. . . ."

"But?" I said.

She shook her head.

"It didn't," she said.

Her blush had faded. She seemed now to be having an easy conversation with a casual acquaintance about a perfectly pleasant subject. No wonder the praying had worked for a while.

"But what I need you to understand," she said, "is that I love my husband. And he loves me. To find out about me would just kill him."

"I'll try to prevent that," I said.

"Have you made any progress?" she said.

"Not much. Do you ever work out at Pinnacle Fitness?"

She nodded.

"Yes," she said. "I have a membership. Why do you ask?"

"Just looking for a pattern," I said.

"Do you have a picture of him?" she said.

"No."

"I do," she said.

"May I see it?" I said.

"I took it when he was asleep," she said, "with the camera in my telephone."

"He doesn't know?" I said.

"No."

She took an envelope from her purse.

"It's a bit salacious," she said.

"Me, too," I said, and put my hand out.

She smiled brightly again and handed me the envelope. I opened it. In the envelope was a computer printout of a digital photograph of a naked man lying on his back on a bed in what was probably a motel room. It was not my kind of salacious. And even if it had been, Nancy had edited out the groin area with a Magic Marker.

Decorum.

Chapter

················◆◆················

6

ALL OF MY CLIENTS were members of Pinnacle Fitness. Which was a pattern. Which
gave me something to do. Of course they
might also have gone to the same gyne-
cologist, or belonged to the same square-
dance club. But a pattern was a pattern.
And it was better than having nothing to
do. So I walked over to Tremont Street and
took a look.

The club was on the top of a newish
building across Tremont Street from the
Common. Until I was a grown man, I had
never even been in any place as glossy as

Pinnacle Fitness. It was a monument to the fitness illusion that somehow working out was fun and glamorous. I thought about the gyms where I'd trained as a kid, when I was a fighter. I had started in Boston at Henry Cimoli's decrepit dump on the waterfront, when the waterfront was decrepit. Henry used to say the location was perfect for screening out the frauds, because only a legitimate tough guy would dare to go down there. Then the waterfront yuppified and so did Henry, and when I went there now I felt sort of misanthropic for not wearing spandex. But there are things that can't be compromised. I refused to dress up to work out.

The lobby of Pinnacle Fitness had sofas and coffee tables and a snack bar where you could get juices and smoothies and tofu sandwiches on seven-grain bread. It was probably not a good place to get a linguica sandwich. I went to the front desk.

"Gary Eisenhower here?" I said.

The young woman at the front desk had a blond ponytail and very white teeth. She was wearing a white polo shirt with the club logo on it and black satin workout pants.

"Excuse me?" she said.

"Gary Eisenhower," I said. "Is he here?"

"Does he work here?"

"I don't know," I said.

She frowned cutely.

"I don't believe we have anyone by that name working here," she said.

"Oh," I said. "Good. So he's a member, then?"

"I, ah, I don't recognize the name," she said.

"Could you look him up for me?" I said.

"I . . . I'm sure the client-services manager can help you," the young woman said. "That's her office right there."

The client-services manager had an open-door policy. I knocked on the open door and she turned in her swivel chair and smiled at me radiantly and stood. She, too, had a blond ponytail and very white teeth. But she was wearing a white top and a black skirt. The skirt was short, and there was a lot of in-shape leg showing between the hem and the top of her black boots.

"Hi, I'm Margi," she said. "How can I help you?"

"I'm looking for Gary Eisenhower," I said.

"Is he a member here?" Margi said.

"That's what I was going to ask you," I said.

"Why do you wish to know?" Margi said.

"I'd like to get in touch with him," I said.

"It is club policy, sir, not to give out member information."

"Something illicit going on here?" I said.

"Of course not," Margi said. "It is simply that we respect our members' privacy."

"Me, too," I said. "So he is a member?"

Margi was getting brisker by the minute; no wonder she made client-services manager.

"I didn't say that, sir."

"Of course not," I said. "But if he's not a member, then there's no privacy issue, is there."

"Of course not," Margi said. "May I ask why you are interested?"

"So what you can do is check your membership records, and if he is not a member, you can tell me."

She frowned. The reasoning had become too convoluted for her. I thought her frown was even perkier than the one I'd seen at the front desk. But I feared that she would never advance beyond client services.

"Are you some kind of policeman or something?" she said.

"I am," I said.

I used to be a policeman, and "or something" covers a lot.

"I don't mean to give you grief, Margi. Just check. If he's not a member, tell me and I'll move on," I said.

I was interested as well as to what she'd do if he was a member.

She looked at me, still frowning, giving it as much thought as she was able. Then she heaved a big sigh and turned to her computer.

"Eisenhower," she said. "Does that start with an I?"

"E," I said, and spelled it for her.

She clicked at her computer for a little while, and then I could see her face relax.

"We have no one by that name as a member," she said.

She could have been lying to get rid of me. But I didn't think she was smart enough to fake the look of relief when she didn't find him. I thanked her.

"Could I buy you a linguica sandwich?" I said.

She looked horrified.

"On Portuguese sweet bread?" I said.

"No," she said, and smiled at me brightly. "But thanks for asking."

Chapter

❖

7

IT WAS NEARLY NOVEMBER. Baseball season was over. And the wind off the Charles River was beginning to have an edge. I was at my desk, with my feet up, thinking about pattern, when two men came in without knocking and closed the door behind them. I opened the right-hand drawer on my desk. The bigger of the two was bald, with biceps that strained against the sleeves of a shiny leather jacket. The other guy was slim and dark, with deep-set eyes and graceful hands.

"Lemme guess," I said. "You're George, and you're Lenny."

The muscular guy looked at the slim guy.

"He's being a wiseass," the dark, slim guy said.

"Maybe he should stop," the muscle guy said.

There was scar tissue around his eyes, and his nose was flat and thick.

"You used to be a fighter?" I said to him.

"Yeah."

"You any good?"

"I look like I was any good?" he said.

"No," I said.

"Do a lot better outside the ring," he said.

The slim, dark guy said, "Shut up, Boo."

" 'Boo'?" I said.

The dark, slim guy looked at me.

"He's Boo," the dark, slim guy said. "I'm Zel. Why you interested in Gary Eisenhower?"

"Why do you ask?" I said.

"Guy I work for wants to know," Zel said.

"Who is he?" I said.

Zel nodded quietly to himself, as if confirming a suspicion.

"Yeah," he said. "That's how it nearly always goes."

"How's that?" I said.

"Everybody's a wiseguy," Zel said. "Everybody's a tough guy."

"Must be disappointing for you," I said.

"That's what Boo's for," he said.

"Glad he's for something," I said.

Zel nodded again in the same sad way.

"So what's your interest in Gary Eisenhower?"

"Who wants to know?"

Zel shrugged.

"Okay," he said. "Boo?"

Boo smiled happily and started around my desk. I took a gun out of my open desk drawer and pointed it at both of them. Boo stopped. He looked disappointed.

"I got one of those, too," Zel said.

"But yours is under your coat," I said.

"True," Zel said. "Back off, Boo."

Boo looked more disappointed, but he stepped back in front of the desk.

"Hard on Boo," Zel said. "He gets all juiced to smack somebody around and then he can't."

"Loving your work is a good thing," I said. "Maybe another time."

"You think you can handle Boo?" Zel said.

"Sure," I said.

"Without the piece?" Zel said.

"Yeah," I said.

"I heard you were good," Zel said.

Boo stared at me. Apparently, he hadn't heard that. Or it hadn't impressed him.

"Kind of like to watch," Zel said. "You decide to try it."

"Been a while," I said, "since I had a fight to prove I could."

"Yeah, I know," Zel said. "Seems kind of pointless, don't it."

"Tiring, too," I said.

"Boo ain't to that point yet," Zel said.

"Probably won't get there soon," I said.

"'Less he starts losing a few," Zel said.

"You want to know my interest in Eisenhower. I want to know who wants to know," I said.

"You show me yours, I show you mine?" Zel said.

"Might work," I said.

"And if it don't?" Zel said.

"I could shoot you," I said.

"But you won't," Zel said.

"Probably not," I said. "Unless Boo becomes a distraction."

Zel nodded. He looked at me for a while. Then he nodded to himself slowly.

"I work for a guy name of Chester Jackson," Zel said.

"What's his interest?" I said.

"Don't know," Zel said. "Show me yours."

"Guy is blackmailing a group of women he had affairs with," I said. "They want me to make him stop."

"Who are the women?"

"Nope," I said.

Zel nodded.

After a while he said, "I think Mr. Jackson will want to talk with you."

"Sure," I said.

Zel took a business card out of his shirt pocket and put it on my desk. Chester Jackson had offices at International Place. I picked up the card and put it in my shirt pocket.

"Chester married?" I said.

Zel shrugged.

"Maybe to a younger woman?" I said.

Zel smiled faintly and shrugged again.

"I'll stop by," I said.

Zel nodded.

"Adiós," he said. "Come on, Boo."

They walked out. At the door Boo turned and looked at me hard.

"I ain't forgetting you," he said.

"Few people do," I said.

Chapter

⸰◆⸰

8

THE SECRETARY HAD a British accent. She ushered me in to see Mr. Jackson as though it was an audience. We were high up. There was the usual spectacular view of the harbor. And in front of the view, on a credenza, was a big photograph of Beth. Chet stood up and came around his desk when I came in.

"Chet Jackson," he said, and put out his hand.

He had a big chin and short black hair with a lot of gray showing. The hair was receding from his forehead. His face was unlined. He smelled of very good cologne.

His grip was strong. He had on a blue suit with a blue-and-white striped tie against a gleaming white shirt. There was a white handkerchief in his breast pocket.

I sat. He sat.

"Coffee?" he said. "Tea? water? Something stronger?"

"No, thanks."

Chet nodded decisively.

"Okay," he said. "What can you tell me about Gary Eisenhower?"

"He's blackmailing a number of women," I said. "They asked me to find him and make him stop."

"Have you found him?"

"No."

"But you've been looking for him at Pinnacle Fitness," Chet said.

"Yes."

"Why?"

"Thought I might find him there," I said.

"What made you think that?"

"Probably," I said, "same thing that made you go there."

"What makes you think I went there?"

"I'm a trained investigator," I said. "One day I ask about Eisenhower there, next day Zel and Boo come around."

"Who are these women who employed you?"

I shook my head.

"I am a man of considerable leverage," Chet said.

"How nice for you," I said.

"And I don't like flippant," Chet said.

"What a shame," I said.

Chet swiveled in his chair and with his back to me looked out his window at his view. After a suitable pause he swiveled back and looked hard at me.

"I want to know who you represent," he said. "And I want to know what led you to Pinnacle."

"I'll be damned," I said. "That's pretty much what I want to learn from you."

We sat silently then, looking at each other. Then Chet smiled at me.

"You're not scared of me, are you?" he said.

"I'm trying to be," I said.

Chet leaned back in his chair a little and laughed.

"Goddamn it," he said. "I like your style."

"That's grand," I said.

We sat again.

I looked around the office.

"What do you do for a living?" I said.

"I make money," Chet said.

"How?" I said.

"Little of this," Chet said. "Little of that."

"Folks that employ people like Zel and Boo," I said, "and make their money by doing a little of this, a little of that, most of those folks have offices in the back of billiard parlors."

"I played football at Harvard," Chet said.

"Wow," I said.

Chet was rubbing his chin with the palm of his left hand.

"Okay," he said. "I'm going to take a chance on you."

He nodded at the picture of Beth on the credenza.

"That's my wife," he said. "Beth. I think she's been involved with Eisenhower."

"Uh-huh," I said.

"Can you confirm or deny that?" Chet said.

"Nope."

"Is she one of your clients?"

I shook my head.

"You wouldn't tell me if she was," Chet said. "Would you?"

I shook my head.

"Can you tell me anything?"

"I figured Gary had a plan ahead of time," I said. "All the women I represent have a common pattern. Young, older husbands of significant wealth. And all of them belonged to Pinnacle Fitness."

Chet nodded.

"Beth belongs," he said.

I nodded. He stopped rubbing his chin and massaged his forehead with both hands for a minute. Then he put his hands flat on his desktop and leaned a little toward me.

"I'm a tough guy," he said. "I make a lot of money in a lot of different ways, and none of the ways is easy."

I nodded.

"I don't mind that," he said. "I don't care too much about too many things. People get in my way, I don't mind moving them out of the way."

I nodded.

"But this is hard," he said.

I was sick of nodding, so I just waited.

"And the reason it's hard is that I made a mistake."

He paused and looked at the back of his hands on the desktop, and breathed a couple of times.

"I let myself love Beth," he said.

"Opens you up a little," I said. "Doesn't it."

"Chink in the armor," he said. "But there it is. I'm fifty-eight. She's thirty. I'm in good shape and all. But I'm almost twice her age."

I went back to nodding.

"We were fine until I began to get a sense that she might be seeing somebody else. No real evidence, little stuff, mostly sort of a feeling. I guess if your wife is cheating on you, at some level, you know."

"If you let yourself," I said.

"After a while I let myself," he said. "I put Zel on her, see what he could find out."

"She doesn't know Zel?" I said.

"No. She doesn't know anything to do with my business."

"Makes it easier," I said.

"Zel's good at things," Chet said. "He tailed her and found out that she was seeing somebody and what his name was." Chet shook his head. "If that's his real name."

"And you started looking into places she might have met him," I said.

"Zel did, yeah. Health club, country club, restaurants, couple of stores on Newbury Street."

"And he didn't find Eisenhower," I said.

"But he established an, ah, relationship with various people to report if anything about Eisenhower surfaced. So when I showed up at Pinnacle Fitness, asking about him . . ."

"We heard about it," Chet said. "And I asked Zel to check it out with you."

"What's your plan if you find Gary Eisenhower."

"I'll have him in for a talk," Chet said.

"How far will you go?" I said.

"Do you mean will I kill him?" Chet said. "I don't think that would get me where I want to get."

"Which is?"

"With Beth, and nobody else."

"And if you aced him, she'd suspect."

"Wouldn't you?" Chet said.

"You're not the only aggrieved husband," I said.

"But you'd be suspicious, wouldn't you?"

"Yeah," I said. "Have you spoken to your wife about any of this?"

"No."

"Might be a good thing," I said.

"Might be," he said.

"But?"

"But I can't," he said. "I simply goddamn can't."

I nodded.

"The best moments in my life," I said, "have come because I loved somebody."

"Yeah," he said.

"And the worst," I said.

"Yeah," he said.

Chapter

❖❖

9

I SAT IN THE client-membership offices with a young woman named Courtney and signed up for a six-month membership at Pinnacle Fitness. I didn't see Margi from the client-services office. Though Courtney could have been Margi with a change of makeup. Then the client-training director took me to the client-training office to assess me physically. He took my blood pressure and pulse. He weighed me. And pronounced me fit. He turned me over to a personal trainer, an in-shape young man named Luke, who offered to help me learn the various pieces of equipment. I declined.

"I've worked out a lot," I said. "I'll be okay on my own."

Luke nodded.

"I kind of figured that," he said. "You need anything, give me a shout."

I got a locker and a padlock. I didn't really need one, except for the gun. I hated wearing a gun while working out. So I changed into some sweats and left the gun in the locker. If Margi spotted me from the client-services office and rushed me, I might be able to run for it.

I was limited in my workouts by the fact that I could use only equipment near the front window, where I could watch for Gary Eisenhower entering the lobby. Who kept not showing up every day.

Susan came with me for a guest workout one day. Everything she wore to work out in fit her exactly and matched perfectly. Her thick, dark hair was held in place by what must have been a designer headband. And her makeup was impeccable. She'd been doing a lot of power yoga lately, which made her even stronger and more supple than she already was. A lot of people looked at her.

"My," Susan said, as she looked around

Pinnacle Fitness. "You fit in here like a rhinoceros at a petting zoo."

"I'm undercover," I said, "disguised as a thug."

"It's very convincing," Susan said. "You're waiting for Gary Whosis to show up?"

"Yes."

"How long do you plan to wait?"

"I have a six-month membership," I said.

"You are a stubborn boy," she said.

"I am."

"Maybe I can help," she said. "Show me the picture again."

"It's still censored," I said.

"How too bad," Susan said.

We worked out as long as we could stand to and then went to change. When I came dressed from the shower, through the front window of the gym I saw Zel and Boo come into the club lobby. I went out.

"Looking for somebody?" I said.

"Same as you," Zel said.

Behind him, Boo was giving me the dead-eye stare that was supposed to freeze my blood in my veins.

I said, "How ya doin', Boo?"

"Fuck you," he said.

I nodded.

"You looking for Gary Eisenhower?" I said to Zel.

"Yep."

"But you don't know what he looks like," I said. "So actually you swung by to see if I'd made any progress."

"Yep," Zel said.

"I haven't," I said.

"You know what he looks like?" Zel said.

"No," I said.

"The hell you don't," Zel said. "You wouldn't be here if you didn't know."

I shrugged.

"How about it, Zel," Boo said. "Lemme go with him a little."

Zel ignored him.

"We're after the same thing," Zel said. "Don't see why we can't cooperate."

"What's Boo after?" I said.

"Boo wants what I want," Zel said.

"And you want?"

"What Chet tells me," Zel said.

"Too many levels of command for me," I said. "I think I'll mosey along on this by myself."

"Don't mind if we mosey on along behind you," Zel said.

"Nope."

"What if you did mind?" Boo said. "What you gonna do?"

"Let's wait until I mind," I said.

Boo wanted so badly to prove he was tougher than I was that I felt almost bad for him.

"Two things, Boo," Zel said. "One, it ain't time for you to do your thing. And two, I ain't so sure you can do it with him."

"Like hell," Boo said.

"Listen to Zel," I said to Boo.

"See you around," Zel said.

He jerked his head toward the elevator. Boo was still giving me the stare.

"Boo," Zel said quietly. "We're leaving."

He walked to the elevator and pushed the button. Boo stared at me. The elevator arrived and the door slid open.

"Boo," Zel said. "Now!"

Boo turned and went to the elevator. Zel followed him in. The door slid shut. I looked back toward the health club. Susan, showered, made up, coiffed, and in street clothes, was standing inside the big window holding a two-and-a-half-pound dumbbell. I went back inside the club.

"What was your plan?" I said.

"The ugly guy you were having a stare-off with," Susan said. "If things unraveled, I was going to run out and hit him with the dumbbell."

"Appropriate choice of weapon," I said.

"For either one of you," Susan said.

I crooked my arm for her to take.

"Buy you a drink, Wonder Woman?" I said.

She took my arm.

"Maybe two," she said.

Chapter

❖❖

10

I WENT EVERY DAY to Pinnacle Fitness. I had to be careful. If I improved my body further, the paparazzi would begin following me. So I worked out sparingly and spent a lot of time watching the snugly dressed young women, looking for exercise tips. I was in my second week at Pinnacle when one of the female trainers walked up to me and put her hand out.

"Hi," she said. "I'm Estelle. Can I help you with your training?"

We shook hands. She had shiny black hair, worn long and straight. There was something faintly Asian-Pacific about her appearance, though it was too faint to tell me what.

"No, thanks," I said. "I don't think anyone can."

She smiled warmly.

"I don't believe that," she said. "If you need anything, please let me know."

I said, "Okay, Estelle."

Since I'd joined no one had spoken to me like that. Why now? I glanced through the front window at the lobby. Across the lobby at the snack bar, a man wearing an ankle-length black overcoat was sipping a smoothie, the healthy devil. He had a short beard and aviator-style sunglasses, and a bright blue silk scarf hanging open around his neck. He didn't seem to be paying attention. Estelle paid me no more attention, either. When he finished his smoothie, the guy in the overcoat left. Sleuthing makes you suspicious. The guy hadn't been in the club. Had he really come up to the top floor of the building to drink a smoothie?

When I was through for the day, I took the elevator down and went out onto Tremont Street. The guy in the overcoat was sitting on a bench across the street at the edge of the Common, reading a newspaper, digesting his smoothie. He fit the physical description of Gary Eisenhower, as best I could tell. But the beard and the sunglasses made it a little hard to judge the face from this distance. If only his loins were blacked out with Magic Marker.

I crossed with the light and headed on down across the Common. Overcoat fell in behind me, at a distance. Even if I hadn't started thinking about him in the health club lobby, I would have made him when he started tailing me. His elaborate lack of interest in me was classic overacting. We crossed Charles Street to the Public Garden. It was late afternoon and already dark in the Back Bay. The Public Garden was full of people walking away from work. I angled left through the Public Garden, crossed at Arlington, and went up Boylston Street toward my office. The guy in the overcoat trailed along. I went in the Boylston Street entrance of my building and walked up a flight to my office. Overcoat lingered outside.

In my office I took off my leather jacket,

put on my baseball hat and a black rain-coat, and went down the back stairs, into the alley, and out onto Berkeley to the corner of Boylston. Overcoat was where I thought he'd be, in the lobby of my build-ing, looking at the tenant directory.

I crossed Boylston Street and stood looking in the window of a Starbucks coffee shop. In the reflection I saw him come out of the building. He headed across Boylston on Berkeley Street toward the river. I tailed him down Berkeley, across Newbury, across Commonwealth Ave, to Beacon Street. He turned right, crossed Arlington, and turned into a low apartment building on the river side of Beacon Street, where it was still flat before Beacon Hill began to rise toward the State House. I stood across the street be-hind the black iron fence where it turned the corner at Arlington Street. In another min-ute or so, the lights went on in the second-floor front.

It was raining lightly; there was a mild wind. I felt like a real private eye, stand-ing in the dark, in the city, with my collar pulled up and my hat pulled down. After a while, I walked across to the doorway of the apartment building and read the names under the doorbells. The second floor was E. Herzog.

I lived only a couple of blocks from E. Herzog, so I turned back into the light rain and walked home.

Gee whiz, I thought, *who can you trust.*

Chapter

11

I TAILED HIM for the next couple of days. I thought it might make some sense to see if I could learn anything. And in truth, I was probably showing off a little. When he'd try to tail me, I spotted him at once. I was behind him for the rest of the week and he never knew it. I couldn't wait to tell Susan.

The next day, Wednesday, I called Martin Quirk and asked him if he could run the names Gary Eisenhower and E. Herzog for me.

"You want me to come by and iron yours shirts, too?"

"I know you," I said. "You'd use too much starch."

"I find anything," Quirk said, "I'll let you know."

I spent the rest of Wednesday hanging around Newbury Street, where Gary shopped with a woman I didn't know in a series of shops that didn't have my size. Thursday was spent mostly in the lobby of The Langham Hotel, where Gary spent the afternoon in a room with one woman, and much of the evening in the same room with a different woman. Neither was a client.

Friday I spent the morning outside a boutique hotel near the State House, while Gary spent it in the hotel with a date, not one of my clients. Gary didn't let a lot of grass grow, I had to give him that.

Friday afternoon he did some shopping in Copley Place. I didn't like Copley Place. It was a large mall in the middle of the city, with a lot of marble and high-end shops, anchored at either end by a large hotel. One could come to the hotel and shop in the mall, and never go outside. The drawback was that inside the mall you had no way to know if you were in Chicago, or Houston, or East Lansing, Michigan.

Gary seemed to like it okay. He bought a cashmere topcoat and a twelve-thousand-dollar suit, and a pair of imported shoes, the price of which I didn't catch. Then he went to one of the hotel bars and had drinks with Estelle, the friendly trainer. They spoke at length and quite intensely, and laughed quite often, and when he left her he kissed her good-bye. Then, carrying his purchases, he headed out of Copley Place and on down Boylston Street.

I drifted along behind him as he walked down Boylston from Copley Place. There was a lot of foot traffic in the late afternoon, and I closed it up a little. He turned at Arlington Street, as I had expected, but then he crossed into the Public Garden and walked toward the little bridge that arched over the Swan Boats. Halfway across the bridge he stopped and leaned on the railing and looked down at the still water. The romantic devil just liked to be on the bridge. I understood that. I did, too. The Swan Boats were in dry dock for the winter. But the pond hadn't been drained yet. When I reached him I stopped and leaned on the bridge railing, too. He kept staring at the water.

I said, "Gary Eisenhower, I presume?"

He looked up as if he was startled. Then he began to smile.

"Goddamn," he said. "You're pretty good."

"Everyone says so."

"How'd you know it was me?" he said.

"Got a picture," I said.

"How the hell . . . ?"

"A woman took it while you were sleeping."

"Damn," he said. "Probably used one of those phone cameras."

"Yep."

He grinned wider.

"Fucking technology," he said. "Want to go someplace and have a drink and talk about things?"

"We'd be fools not to," I said.

Chapter

❖❖

12

WE WALKED OVER to the Four Seasons and got a table in The Bristol Lounge. Gary ordered a "Maker's Mark, rocks, water back." I had a beer. Gary put his shopping bags on the floor beside him and unbuttoned his overcoat but didn't take it off. Under the coat he had on a coffee-colored coarse-weave turtleneck sweater. He took a long swallow of his bourbon when it arrived, and sipped a little water.

"Oh, Momma," he said. "Nothing like it when you need it."

"Or even when you don't," I said.

"You got that right," he said.

He looked around.

"Nice room," he said.

"Yes, it is."

"One of the places I bring them," he said.

"Nothing but the best," I said. "You ever pay?"

He grinned at me and sipped more bourbon.

"Not often," he said.

He stirred the remaining bourbon and ice with his forefinger for a moment.

"Nice gig," he said. "I hope we can work something out. I'd hate to give it up."

"Tell me about the gig," I said.

"You probably got most of it figured out," he said.

"Tell me anyway," I said. "I'm much dumber than I seem."

Gary leaned back in his chair and laughed hard.

"Aren't we all," he said.

He drank the rest of his bourbon, spotted the waitress, pointed to the glass. She nodded and looked at me. I shook my head.

"Okay," Gary said. "I'm good with women, you know? They like me. For a while I used that to get a lot of tail."

"Good to have a hobby," I said.

He grinned.

"That's what it was at first, a hobby," he said. "But I like a lot of action."

"And you believe in diversity," I said.

"I do," he said. "And that makes the hobby get kind of expensive."

"Lot of wining and dining before you even get to the hobby part," I said.

"Pretty much at first," Gary said. "After you sort of get established it gets cheaper, you know? You cut out the wining and dining, get right to the hobby."

I nodded. The waitress came with Gary's drink. It made him happy. He drank some of it.

"But one day," I said, "it occurred to you that you might be able to turn the hobby into a living."

He pointed to me.

"Exactly," he said. "You sure you're not smart?"

"Pretty sure," I said.

"I think you're too modest," Gary said.

"That, too," I said. "So how did you do the blackmail?"

"Hey, dude, what a terrible word," he said.

"Okay," I said. "How did you go about professionalizing your hobby?"

"First time I tried it," Gary said, "I rented a motel room for a couple days. I got some software in my computer that allows pictures to be taken through the screen. I set it up focused on the bed, so it looked like it was just on the table, where I'd been typing or something. And I set it to go off every few seconds. As backup, I put a tape recorder under the bed. So when the action started I made sure the positions were right for pictures and sound. It worked. And as time went along, I refined it. Got a tiny video camera, set it up in the corner of the room. In a shadow. Taped sight and sound."

Gary sipped some bourbon. As he swallowed, he held the glass up in front of him and gave it a little kiss.

"In some ways, the sound is better than the pictures," he said.

"But harder to identify," I said.

"Yeah. That's why you need the pictures. But the stuff they said . . ." He shook his head. "You know how a lot of women say stuff during sex?"

"I recall something about that," I said.

"You married?" Gary said.

"No, but I'm with the girl of my dreams," I said.

"Girl of your dreams?" Gary said.

"Uh-huh."

"She say stuff?"

I didn't say anything.

Gary shrugged.

"À chacun son goût," he said.

"Oui," I said.

He grinned.

"Anyway, I got some excellent action," he said. "Some of it pretty kinky."

I nodded.

"You want to hear about it?" Gary said.

"Another time," I said.

"You got a problem with kinky, Spense?"

"Not among consenting adults," I said. "And don't call me Spense."

"Oh, sure, apologize," he said. "Anyway, it was duck soup. So I started doing it regular. I made sure the women were married and had money, preferably married to older rich men, so they might be looking for action but would never want to give up the husband and his money."

"Estelle help you with that?" I said.

"Boy, you don't miss much," Gary said. "How'd you know that?"

"She fingered me for you," I said.

"Oh," he said. "Yeah."

"She'd have access to the membership records," I said.

"She does," Gary said. "She knows what we're looking for."

"Many failures?" I said.

"Now and then," Gary said. "Not as often as you'd think."

He was a very handsome man. Six feet tall, maybe a little more, wide shoulders, narrow hips, good color, dressed like a male model.

"She doesn't mind you having sex with all these women?" I said.

"I think she likes it," he said.

I nodded.

"So how often do you practice your, ah, profession," I said.

"It's still a hobby, too," Gary said. "I do it every day."

"Why?" I said.

"Why?"

"Yeah," I said. "Why?"

"'Cause I can, for crissake."

"Well," I said, "it's nice to like your work."

Chapter

❖❖

13

GARY WAS ON HIS THIRD bourbon. But it was going in much more slowly, and he showed little effect from the first two. I had my second beer.

"So where do we stand?" Gary said.

"What's the E stand for," I said.

"E?"

"As in E. Herzog."

Gary looked at me for a long moment.

"Oh, shit," he said.

I waited.

After a while, Gary grinned at me.

"Okay," he said. "You're smart. That dumb stuff is just a ploy."

"Maybe," I said. "But what I've done so far doesn't prove anything."

"You think?" he said.

"Your big mistake was trying to tail me. If you hadn't made it, I would have had a much harder time finding you."

"You spotted me following you the other day and turned it around and followed me."

"Yep."

Gary shook his head.

"Amateurs and professionals, huh?"

"What's the E stand for?" I said.

"Elliot," he said.

"Is Elliot Herzog your real name?" I said.

Again, Gary grinned at me.

"One of them," he said.

I nodded.

"So what are your plans," I said, "for the ladies who employed me?"

He smiled.

"Abigail, Beth, Nancy, Regina," he said. "The gang of four."

"Are they the only ones with whom you are at the moment practicing your profession?"

"Not hardly," Gary said.

"Maybe you should plan to stick with them," I said. "And leave my gang alone."

He picked up a butter knife and tapped a little beat on the table with it while he looked at me.

"I got no reason to change my plans," he said.

"I'm supposed to give you a reason," I said.

He shrugged.

"What are you gonna do?" he said. "These ladies are willing to pay because they don't want their husbands to know. That hasn't changed. None of them will press charges. If you tell the cops or whatever, every one of them will deny that they ever had anything to do with me."

"I could keep punching your lights out," I said, "until we reach an agreement."

"Yeah, maybe," he said. "I have a sense that it might not be your style. But say it was. If you did it once, okay, I'm sore for a few days. I might be tougher than you think I am. And when I felt better, I'd get hold of your employers and they'd call you off, for fear I'd expose them."

"And if they didn't?" I said.

"I'd expose them," he said. "They're not the only fish in my creel, you know?"

"I don't seem to terrify you," I said.

"I been living this life for a long time," he said. "I'm pretty light on my feet."

"And the cops don't terrify you," I said.

"Nothing much does," he said. "You got the tab on this?"

"Sure," I said. "Expense account."

"Sort of like me," he said, and stood up.

"See you around," he said.

"Yep," I said.

He picked up his shopping bags and strolled out of the lounge. I watched him go and smiled. I kind of liked him. I picked up his butter knife by the blade and slipped it into my coat pocket. Then I paid the bill, tipped handsomely, and strolled out of the lounge, too.

Chapter

❖

14

GOT SIX E. HERZOGS," Quirk said to me. "None of them named Elliot. Got no Gary Eisenhowers."

"There's a surprise," I said.

We were having lunch at Locke-Ober.

"How come you know everybody?" I said.

"Been coming here a long time, most of them are politicians or lawyers."

"That you met in your work," I said.

"Yep," Quirk said.

He grinned.

"Arrested some of them," he said.

"Not enough," I said.

"Everybody got arrested that should get arrested," Quirk said, "we wouldn't have no place to put them."

"How about the butter knife?" I said.

Quirk nodded.

"There were prints on the butter knife," he said. "Yours were on the blade, and there were two others."

"One would be whoever set the table," I said.

"Young woman named Lucille Malinkowski," Quirk said.

"Why have you got her prints on file?"

"Don't know, nothing criminal. Maybe she was in the army, maybe she has a gun license, maybe she used to work someplace where she had to have clearance. I didn't know you'd care."

"And the other one?

"Belongs to a guy named Goran Pappas," Quirk said.

"'Goran'?"

"Aka Gary Pappas," Quirk said.

"Why is Gary in the system," I said.

"He did three in MCI-Shirley for swindling," Quirk said.

"From a woman?" I said.

"Yes."

"What'd Gary look like?" I said.

"Six feet one inch, one hundred seventy pounds, dark hair, brown eyes, even features, age thirty-eight at the time of his arrest."

"Which was?"

"In 2002," Quirk said.

He produced a computer printout of Gary Pappas's mug shot. It was Gary Eisenhower.

"Anybody want him now for anything?" I said.

"He's not in the system," Quirk said. "Course, the system's imperfect."

"It is?" I said. "How did that happen?"

Quirk didn't bother to answer.

"You want to discuss Gary with me?" he said.

"He's blackmailing a bunch of women," I said.

"Tell me about it," Quirk said.

I told him most of it, leaving out the names.

"Not a bad gig," Quirk said. "Banging good-looking women every day, getting money for it."

"It might get boring," I said.

Quirk looked at me.

"Or not," I said.

Quirk nodded.

"So they hired you to make him stop," Quirk said.

"Yes."

"You got any evidence?" Quirk said.

"Got no evidence we can use."

"Women won't testify?"

"No."

"So what are you supposed to do?" Quirk said. "Scare him?"

"I tried that," I said.

"How'd that work for you?" Quirk said.

"It didn't," I said.

"Disappointing," Quirk said.

"Makes me feel old," I said.

"Want me to stop by and have a talk with him?" Quirk said. "Unofficially?"

I shook my head.

"Don't think he'd care," I said.

"About the homicide commander?" Quirk said.

"I don't think cops worry him," I said.

"Now I feel old," Quirk said.

"This is a pretty cool guy," I said. "He knows what he's doing, and he doesn't seem to scare."

"Like you and me," Quirk said.

"Yeah, but he's better-looking," I said.

"Than you and me?" Quirk said. "How is that possible?"

Chapter

............•◆•............

15

SUSAN AND I made love on Sunday morning
at her place with the bedroom door closed
and Pearl grumbling unhappily outside it.
When we were through, Susan whisked the
covers up over us, as she always did, and
we lay quietly on the bed for a while.

"You know, don't you," Susan said, "that
I was a cheerleader at Swampscott High
School?"

"I do know that," I said.

Susan flipped the covers back and rolled
out of bed, and stood naked beside it.

"Sis-boom-bah," she said, and jumped
into the air and kicked her heels back.

"Is that in honor of my performance?" I said.

"Ours," she said. "And us."

I nodded.

"Sis-boom-bah," I said.

Susan opened the bedroom door and Pearl bounded in, jumped on the bed, turned around maybe fifteen times, and flopped down where Susan had been. I looked at her. Then I looked at Susan.

"There's a definite difference," I said.

"Pearl was never a cheerleader," Susan said.

We showered and dressed, which took me considerably less time than it took Susan. She was just snapping her bra when I headed for the kitchen to start breakfast. Pearl stayed where she was.

By the time I had made my whole-wheat blackberry pancakes and put them on the plates, she came out with her face on and her clothes in place. It was weekend informal, a scoop-neck black T-shirt, jeans, and loafers. But everything fit her so perfectly and she was so beautiful that I felt the same rush of amazement and triumph I always felt in moments like these.

She sat at the table and sipped her

orange juice. I put the pot of coffee on the table and sat across from her and looked at her. She looked back at me, and finished her orange juice, and said something that sounded like "hum," which I knew to be positive. I drank some orange juice and poured us some coffee. Pearl sat attentively beside the table. I would have been quite willing to discuss the particulars of what Susan and I had just done together, but I knew it violated some inward standard of privacy that she maintained. Sex is good; talking about it afterward is not good. So I shut up. Shutting up rarely leads to anything bad.

"I was thinking about your person," she said.

"You're my person," I said.

"No, no, I mean the Gary Eisenhower person. Did you tell me he has sex every day?"

"Seems to," I said.

"With people he doesn't love," she said.

"That's my impression," I said.

"What do you think of that?" she said.

"Sounds great," I said. "But, present company excluded, of course, it is really an adolescent fantasy, which, humor aside, most adult men would get bored with."

"Would you?"

"Yes," I said.

"With me?" she said.

"Never been tested."

"Do you think we make love enough?" Susan said.

"Yes," I said. "And very high quality."

She nodded and took a small bite of pancake.

"Yum," she said. "Blackberries."

"Did I pass?" I said.

"Pass?"

"The little quiz you just gave me," I said. "Did I pass?"

She smiled.

"Yes," she said. "But I was actually thinking about Gary Whosis."

"You think he wouldn't pass?"

"I think if he does in fact have sex with as many women as often as he does, that there's something more than simple pleasure."

"That would be true of us," I said.

"That our sex life is about more than simple pleasure?"

"Yes."

"True, and what is it?"

I grinned at her.

"Love?"

"That would be my guess," Susan said.

I grinned at her.

"Sis-boom-bah!" I said.

Chapter

❖

16

WE WERE ALL in the conference room again, me, Elizabeth Shaw, and the gang of four, as Gary had named them.

"His real name is Goran Pappas," I said. "He also uses the name Elliot Herzog. He lives on Beacon Street, just before it climbs the hill. He's done time for swindling. He appears to have preselected you, using information provided him by a woman at the health club. There appear to be other women in his life beyond you four."

"His name is Goran?" Regina said.

"He uses the nickname Gary," I said.

"Gary Pappas?" she said.

"How'd you find all this out?" Abigail Larson said.

"Amazing, isn't it?"

"No, really, how do you know?" Abigail said.

I looked inscrutable.

"Vee haf our vays," I said.

"It seems to me our next question," Elizabeth said, "is now that we have him located, what steps can we take to contain him?"

The women looked at one another. Then they all looked at me.

"What should we do?" Nancy said.

"He's a blackmailer," I said. "We could arrest him."

"Would we have to testify?" Nancy said.

"Yes."

Abigail looked at Elizabeth.

"Is that true?"

"You're the victims," Elizabeth said. "You'd have to make the complaint. You'd have to testify in court, if the case went there. We could probably keep it fairly low-key, with luck."

"But my husband would have to know," Nancy said.

"Very likely," Elizabeth said.

"Then I won't do it," Nancy said.

I looked around the room. All of the women were shaking their heads.

"Couldn't you just make him stop?" Regina said. "You know, beat him up or something?"

"Several things against that," I said. "One, I don't like doing it. Two, it's illegal. Three, I believe that if I did, he'd blow the whistle on you."

"Blow the whistle?" Abigail said.

"Send evidence of your infidelity to your husbands," I said.

Everybody sat. No one said anything. Everybody looked at one another.

Finally Regina said in a very soft voice, "Could you kill him?"

"No," I said.

"Do you know someone who would?" she said.

"Yes."

"Could you get him to do it?"

"No," I said.

"But why?" Regina said.

"That's enough," Elizabeth said. "There will be no more talk of that nature from any of you, if you wish me to continue as your attorney."

Everyone was quiet, as if they'd been chastised by the teacher.

"I could try to arrange some kind of pay-off," I said.

"He wants so much," Beth said.

"How much?"

"Twenty-five thousand dollars a month," Beth said.

"From each of you?"

The other women nodded.

"I have access to some money of my own. Chet is very generous," Beth said. "But I can't keep paying out that kind of money without eventually having to turn to him."

The other women nodded in agreement.

"Can you come up with one big payoff?" I said. "I might be able to persuade him to take it and move on, rather than have me on his case all the time."

"I can't without Chet knowing," Beth said.

"Me, either," Abigail said.

The two others shook their heads. I looked at Elizabeth.

"Counselor?" I said.

"I'm a trust lawyer," she said. "I don't know what we should do."

I stood up.

"Good luck," I said.

Nobody said anything, but they all looked at me mournfully as I moved toward the door. I shrugged.

"Can't win 'em all," I said.

Chapter

⸭

17

HAWK AND I were having a "Thank God it's late Thursday afternoon" drink at the far end of the bar in Grill 23.

"What's the book?" I said to Hawk.

He looked at the hardcover on the bar beside him. The flap was keeping his place about one hundred pages in.

"New one by Janet Evanovich," he said.

"Good?"

"Course it's good. Would I be reading it, it's not good?"

"You reading it, it wouldn't dare," I said.

Hawk smiled.

"Don't suppose you want me to pop Gary Eisenhower for you," Hawk said.

"There's nothing going on here," I said, "that anyone should die for."

"Just an offer," Hawk said.

"Thanks," I said.

Hawk sipped some champagne.

"What are friends be for," he said, "they can't scrag somebody for you now and then?"

"I'll take a raincheck," I said.

Hawk looked as he always did, as if he'd just been washed and polished. His clothes were immaculate. His shirt seemed to glow with whiteness. His shaved head gleamed in the bar's light.

"Maybe I should shave my head," I said.

"White guys don't look good with their heads shaved," Hawk said.

"Why is that?" I said.

"Don't know," Hawk said. "Don't look as good with hair, either."

"Are you making invidious racial comparisons?" I said.

"Uh-huh," Hawk said.

The bartender came down the bar and replaced our drinks.

"You say he knew the names of the women hired you," Hawk said.

"Yes."

"How many women he working, you think?"

"More than four," I said.

"So somebody tole him," Hawk said.

"Be my guess," I said.

"One of them don't believe she ain't special to him," Hawk said.

"You know this how?" I said.

"Simplest explanation," he said.

"True," I said.

"People believe what they need to believe," Hawk said.

"Also true," I said.

Hawk sipped his champagne. I had a little scotch.

"I got nowhere to go," I said. "No one will testify, no one will bargain with him. They all want something they can't have."

"And there's a lot you don't know," Hawk said.

"Susan says there's something wrong with Gary," I said. "That he has as much sex as he does, with various women about whom he doesn't care very much."

"Strange tail," Hawk said.

"I know," I said. "I'm not sure Susan gets that, exactly."

"She gets most things," Hawk said.

"She does," I said.

"I been thinking 'bout cutting back myself," Hawk said.

"Official male attitudes aside, is there such a thing as too much sex?"

"Sure," Hawk said.

"Even at your tolerance level?" I said.

"Even then," Hawk said.

"So what does that do for me?" I said.

"You the sleuth," Hawk said. "I just a simple negro man."

"Simple," I said.

Hawk was looking down the bar at a woman in a dark blue suit.

"Attractive to women, though," he said.

"I thought she was looking at me," I said.

"She not," Hawk said.

I sipped some scotch.

"I suppose I could go back a little, get a little history on Gary," I said.

"He done a triple at Shirley?" Hawk said.

I nodded.

"For swindling some woman?"

I nodded.

"Might make sense to talk to the woman," Hawk said.

"I'm a man of great intellectual curiosity," I said.

We finished our second round. The bartender delivered a third.

"You sure that woman isn't looking at me?" I said.

"What you care?" Hawk said. "You don't fool around no more."

I grinned at him.

"I was never fooling," I said.

Chapter

18

I WAS IN MY OFFICE, at my desk, looking at Gary Pappas's full folder that Quirk had gotten for me. Susan was at a conference in Portland, Maine, and wouldn't be back until tomorrow. So Pearl was on the couch in my office, which had been purchased for her use. Though now and then, when she wasn't around, Susan and I used it for our own purposes. My office door opened softly. Pearl barked. My visitors hesitated.

"It's all right, she won't bite you," I said.

The door opened wider and in came Regina Hartley with a man. Pearl barked again, and they looked at me. Pearl had not bothered to get off the couch and remained prone while she barked.

"It's Bring Your Dog to Work Day," I said. "Have a seat."

They walked cautiously past her and sat in front of my desk. Pearl rested her head on her paws and murmured threateningly. I looked at her. She stopped.

"This is my husband, Clifford," Regina said.

"How do you do?" I said, master of the *bon mot.*

"We need your help," Regina said.

"Haven't done much for you so far," I said.

"This isn't about the other girls," Regina said. "This is just about us."

I nodded. She looked at her husband. He looked at me. I waited.

"This is awkward," he said.

"I often hear awkward things," I said. "I don't mind."

He was a slim man, very erect, very well dressed in a blue suit with a blue-striped pin-collar shirt. His hair was white and close-cut. His color was good. He looked at his wife again.

"I can't," she said.

He nodded and took a deep breath, and went off the high board.

"I'm gay," he said.

"Lot of that going around," I said.

"Regina knows. Has always known," he said. "We care about each other very much, but our lives sometimes run in, ah, separate, though I think parallel, directions."

"And that works for you?"

"Yes," he said. "It does."

Regina nodded.

"Are you out?" I said.

He was silent for a long moment. Then he shook his head.

"No," he said.

"Would being outed do you harm?"

"I fear so," he said. "I am being considered as a candidate for the United States Senate."

"And you fear your gayness would rule you out?"

"Not simply that I am gay," he said, "but that Regina and I have lived separate sexual lives . . . rather, I fear, vigorously."

"Nothing wrong with vigor," I said.

"You see my problem," he said. "If I am

nominated, this Gary Eisenhower is like a loose cannon out there rolling around."

"Does he know?" I said.

"About me?" Clifford said. "No, but he knows about Regina, and when I run, he'll see his big chance, and I'm afraid it will all come out."

"Massachusetts has a pretty good history with gay issues," I said.

"I know," he said. "But it's not just gay issues. My wife has slept with an assortment of men." He smiled faintly. "And so have I."

I nodded.

"Not a matter of one boyfriend," I said.

"No," Clifford said.

I looked at Regina. She shrugged.

"No," she said.

I nodded.

"Why did you join with the other women?" I said to Regina.

"I thought maybe it would work," she said. "That we could find someone to make him go away."

"Can you keep paying him?" I said.

"For a while," Clifford said. "But it is intolerable."

I nodded.

"You like your life?"

"Yes," he said. "We both do."

Regina nodded.

"I adore her," he said. "We share everything, except sex. I hope to be with her all my life."

"Regina?" I said.

"I feel the same way," she said.

I leaned back in my chair. Pearl snored gently on the couch.

"Then fess up," I said.

"You mean tell everyone?" Regina said. "No! No, no, no!"

"Tell the truth," I said. "And you've taken away his every weapon."

"It would destroy my candidacy," Clifford said.

"Maybe," I said. "Say it did. You'd still have your life."

"No, Clifford," Regina said. "I won't let you do this to us."

"Would you lose your income?" I said.

"I inherited a considerable estate from my father," he said. "Essentially, I manage it."

"So your job is safe."

He smiled faintly again.

"Yes," he said.

I spread my hands and turned both palms up.

"The truth will set you free," I said.

"No," Regina said. "I won't have you do this. We've wanted this for all of our marriage. You cannot give it up now that it's so close."

I looked at him.

"She's right," he said. "I can't give it up. Not now. For both our sakes."

I didn't say anything.

"Can't you think of anything to do?" Regina said.

I looked at Pearl. She was asleep upside down with her feet draped over the back of the couch and her head hanging off. She appeared not to have thought of anything, either.

"Not yet," I said.

Chapter

◆◆

19

"I SEE IT ALL THE TIME in my patients," Susan said. "There is a way to save themselves and they won't take it. Can't take it."

We had a table by the window at Sorellina. Susan was sipping a martini, up with olives. I had a Dewar's and soda. I was sipping, too. It was just that my sips were much bigger than Susan's.

"Hell," I said. "If their fears are realized, he'll lose the nomination anyway."

"It's too bad," Susan said. "They seem to have achieved a life many people wish they could have. They have, apparently, a stable, loving relationship and sex lives that fulfill them."

"So they say."

"You don't believe them?" Susan said.

"I don't believe them or not believe them," I said. "We'll see."

"Well, say they are telling the truth," Susan said. "They're together. They have enough money."

"Yep."

"The American dream," Susan said. "Or one version of it."

"Yep."

"But because it's a variation on the tra-ditional dream," Susan said, "this man has the power to destroy them."

"It's a power they've given him," I said.

"What would you do?" Susan said.

"I'd call a press conference. Tell every-body everything, and if they didn't like it they could vote for my opponent."

"But you wouldn't run for political office anyway," Susan said.

"'If nominated I will not run. If elected I will not serve,'" I said.

"Yes," she said.

"How about you?"

"Would I confess to save the life we have?"

"Um-hmm."

"Absolutely."

"And should we live separate sexual lives?" I said.

"Do you want to?" Susan said.

"No."

"Me, either," Susan said.

"So let's not," I said.

"Okay."

She picked up her menu. I had a large sip of my scotch, which emptied the glass. I asked our waiter for more.

"I been reading Gary Eisenhower's folder," I said. "I got it from Quirk. He was blackmailing a woman named Clarice Richardson. They'd had an affair, same MO, pictures, audiotapes."

"Married with a rich husband?" Susan said.

"Married," I said. "But not to a rich man. She was the president of a small liberal-arts college in Hartland. I think it's all women."

"Outside of Springfield?" Susan said.

"Yeah. She was afraid she'd lose her

husband, for whom she cared. And her job, for which she cared."

"I think I'll have the raw tuna," Susan said.

"But she didn't have enough money to keep making her payments."

"So she went to the police?" Susan said.

"And Gary did three in Shirley."

Susan had put her menu down.

"So what happened to her?" Susan said.

"I thought you and I could go out to Hartland and find out."

"You and I?"

"Yeah."

"Will we visit the Basketball Hall of Fame?" Susan said.

"Sure."

"How about the Springfield Armory?" Susan said.

"Absolutely."

"Anything else?"

"When we weren't investigating, and sightseeing," I said, "we could frolic naked in our motel room."

Susan stared at me for a while.

"I am a nice Jewish girl from Swampscott," she said. "I have a Ph.D. from Harvard. Do you seriously think I would wish to frolic naked in a motel room outside of Springfield?"

"How about Chicopee?" I said.

Susan looked at me in silence for a moment while she took another sip of her martini. The she nodded her head slowly and smiled.

"Springfield it is," she said.

Her smile was like sunrise.

Chapter

❖

20

SPRINGFIELD IS A CITY of about 150,000 on the Connecticut River in Western Mass, near the Connecticut line. Hartland is a small town about fifteen miles upriver. We checked in to the William Pynchon Motel on Route 5, outside of Hartland, which made Susan look a little grim.

"I'm not sure about the naked frolicking," she said. "I agreed to Springfield."

"No need to decide now," I said. "Hartland is nice."

We drove into the town to look for Clarice Richardson, the woman who had put Gary Eisenhower in jail.

"Trees," Susan said.

She had the same look of gladiatorial grimness that she'd had looking at the motel. We who are about to die salute you.

"Later we can have lunch," I said. "I spotted a dandy little tearoom."

"Oh, God," Susan said.

Parking in Hartland was not an issue. We left the car right across from the wrought-iron archway that led to the college campus.

"Should we start at the college?" Susan said.

"Don't know where else to start," I said.

"It's breathtaking sometimes," Susan said, "to watch you work."

"It's one of the reasons I brought you," I said. "Give you a chance to watch me in the field."

"The excitement never stops," she said.

We got directions to the president's office and spoke to the secretary in the outer room.

"I'm trying to locate Clarice Richardson," I said.

"Do you have an appointment?" the secretary said.

"With Clarice Richardson?" I said.

"Yes, sir," the secretary said. "Do you have an appointment with President Richardson?"

I took out one of my cards, the plain, elegant one with only my name and address, no crossed pistols, and handed it to her.

"Please tell President Richardson it's about Goran Pappas," I said.

She took my card.

"Please have a seat," she said, and went off down a short corridor.

"Brilliant," Susan said, "how you ran her to ground."

"Who knew," I said.

"Makes me think well of the school," Susan said.

"Yes," I said.

The secretary returned.

"President Richardson will see you shortly," she said, and went back to her desk.

Susan and I sat. The outer office was paneled in oak, with a big working pendulum clock on the wall and a wine-colored Persian rug on the floor.

"You think it's politically correct," I said to Susan, "to call that a Persian rug?"

"Iranian rug doesn't sound right," she said.

"I know."

"How about Oriental?" Susan said. "More general."

"I think Oriental may be incorrect, too," I said.

"How about a big rug from somewhere east of Suez?"

The door opened to the outer office and a strapping woman came in carrying a gun and wearing a uniform with a Hartland College police emblem on the sleeve. She glanced at us and went on down to the president's office, knocked, opened the door, went in, and closed the door.

"She's kind of scary," Susan said.

"Yeah, she's big," I said. "But for simple ferocity, I like your chances."

The secretary stood and said, "President Richardson will see you now."

Chapter

❖

21

CLARICE RICHARDSON stood when we came in. I had no real idea what a standard-issue college president looked like, but I was pretty sure Clarice Richardson wasn't it. She had to be in her early fifties, but she looked ten years younger. She had the kind of patrician face that you see around Harvard Square and Beacon Hill, and sandy hair cut short. She was wearing a cropped black leather jacket over a pencil skirt, black hose, and black boots with two-and-a-half-inch heels. She wore very little jewelry, except for a wedding ring, and her makeup was understated but expert. Especially expert around the eyes. She had big eyes, like Susan, and she crackled with a warm, intelligent sexuality that would call to you across a crowded cocktail party. She wasn't quite Susan, but together in a relatively small room, Susan didn't overpower her.

The big female cop stood against the wall behind and to my right of Clarice's big modern desk. There was a modern credenza in the bay behind the desk, in front of the big picture window. On it were pictures of a gray-haired man with a beard, two young women, and a white bull terrier.

"Mr. Spenser?" Clarice said.

"Yes, ma'am, and this is my associate, Dr. Silverman."

If you have it, you may as well flaunt it.

"Susan," Susan said.

"Really," Clarice said. "Doctor of what, Susan?"

"I have a Ph.D. in psychology," Susan said. "I'm a therapist."

"Where did you do your doctorate?"

"Harvard," Susan said.

"Really? I did, too," Clarice said. "In history. When were you there?"

Susan told her. Clarice shook her head.

"I was there before you," she said.

"But we're both really smart," Susan said.

Clarice smiled.

"We must be," she said, and looked at me. "Because you said you wished to discuss a very charged subject, I have taken the liberty of asking Officer Wysocki to join us."

Officer Wysocki nodded. I nodded back. I had the strong impression she didn't like me.

"May I speak freely?" I said. "President Richardson."

"You may," said Clarice. "And please, call me Clarice."

"I'm a private detective," I said. "In Boston. I was employed recently by a group of women to locate a man who is blackmailing them. He was using the name Gary Eisenhower, but his real name as far as I can tell is Goran Pappas."

"Susan works with you?"

"Susan is with me," I said. "I thought she might be helpful in our conversation. And in truth, when she's not around, I miss her."

Clarice nodded. I looked at the photographs on the credenza.

"Your husband?" I said.

"Yes."

"Your daughters?"

"Yes, and our dog, Cannon. The girls used to call him Cannon Ball, but we shortened it to Cannon."

"And you're all together?" I said.

"Yes," she said.

"And you are still the president of this college," I said.

"Yes."

"So standing up to Pappas may have cost you a lot, but it didn't cost you everything," I said.

"In fact," she said. "It saved everything."

"Good," I said. "Can you tell me about it?"

Clarice looked at Susan.

"He seems an unusual private detective," she said. "Something of a romantic. Should I trust him?"

"Not if you have something you don't want him to know," Susan said.

"Did he bring you along, and tell me he'd miss you if he didn't, to impress me? So I would, so to speak, lower my guard. Or was he sincere?"

"Both," Susan said. "He is romantic. He understands things. And we love one another. But he is also the hardest man I have ever met, when he thinks it's necessary, and I guess you should know that, too."

"Suze," I said. "I didn't bring you along to blow my cover."

Clarice smiled.

"I'm sorry to discuss you like this, as if you were a wall sconce," she said.

"It's okay," I said. "I understand. Harvard girls."

"Exactly," Clarice said.

"Pappas has a hold on a number of people, such as he had on you," I said. "I'm trying to figure how to get them loose."

"Tell the truth," Clarice said.

"They won't."

Clarice nodded.

"It is idle to tell them they should," she said, and looked at Susan. "Is it not, Dr. Silverman?"

"It is," Susan said.

"So if you can tell me what you can about your experience with Pappas," I said, "maybe it'll help."

She nodded.

"Trudy," she said to the big cop. "It's okay, you can go. I'll be fine."

"I can wait outside, Clarice," Trudy said.

"No, thank you, Trudy. Go ahead."

Trudy nodded and looked at me hard and left. Clarice watched her go and then turned in her chair toward me and crossed her legs.

"How shall we begin," she said.

I fought off the urge to say "Start at the beginning."

Instead I said, "Tell it any way that makes sense to you."

She leaned back a little in her chair and looked for a moment at the pictures on her credenza, and took in a long breath and let it out, and said, "Okay."

Chapter

22

MY HUSBAND'S NAME IS ERIC," she said. "Eric Richardson. I met him in graduate school. We've been married for twenty-five years. He is a professor of history at this college."

As she talked I could look past the family pictures and out onto the campus. The day was overcast. No students were in sight. The maple trees had shed their leaves for the season and looked sort of spectral.

"About seven years ago," Clarice said, "for reasons not relevant to this discussion, Eric and I became estranged. We didn't actually separate. But we separated emotionally. I know we loved one another through the whole time, but we also hated each other."

She looked at Susan. Susan nodded.

"The girls were away at school, and we were"—she paused and glanced out the window—"here."

"Not a lot of options here," I said. "If it isn't working at home."

"No," Clarice said. "Though we both sought them."

"And Goran Pappas was one?"

"Yes," she said. "He was calling himself Gary Astor at the time."

"Gary Astor," I said.

She smiled without much pleasure.

"I know," she said. "Pathetic, isn't it?"

"In retrospect," I said.

She held her smile for a moment.

"I was at an alumnae function in Albany," she said, "when I met him in the hotel bar. He was, of course, charming."

She paused again and looked out at the gray campus.

"And I, of course, was starved for charm," she said. "He was relaxed, he was funny, he obviously thought I was wonderful, and sexy, and amazing. We talked all evening and went our separate ways. But we agreed to have drinks the next night, and we did, and then we went to my room."

We were silent for a time. Until Susan spoke.

"And so it began," she said.

Clarice nodded.

"We began to meet regularly at a hotel in Springfield," she said. "Near the Civic Center. It was quite lovely for several months . . . except for the guilt."

Susan nodded.

"And your husband?" Susan said.

"Eric is," Clarice said, "or he was at that time, the kind of man who tends to hunch his shoulders, and lower his head, and wait for the storm to pass."

"So no solace there," Susan said.

Clarice nodded.

"No," she said. "I imagine I would have felt better if he had been unfaithful, too."

Susan nodded slowly.

"I'm sorry, but I need to ask. Is there anything in particular you remember about your relationship?"

"For a while it was a joy."

"How about the, ah, sexual part."

"What I remember most was that he seemed very," she said, "very . . . forceful."

"Cruel?" Susan said.

"No, merely strong and forceful."

"And did things change?" I said.

"Sexually it didn't, until it stopped," she said. "Three months after we met, he showed me his pictures. He played his audiotapes."

She stopped and sat silently for a moment, looking at nothing. I opened my mouth. Susan shook her head. I closed my mouth.

"After a time," Clarice said, "he wanted money or he said he would ruin me. He was pleasant about it, just a simple business transaction, didn't mean we couldn't be friends, or"—she shook her head—"lovers."

"Did you have money?" I said.

"Not enough," she said. "He wanted me to embezzle from the college."

"And you wouldn't," I said.

She shook her head.

"I had cheated enough," she said. "I went to the police."

"In Hartland?"

She smiled.

"No," she said. "State police. They asked me to wear a listening device. I did, and they arrested him. There was some sort of justice, I think, in that. Like hoisting him upon his own petard."

"Then what?" I said.

"Then I told my husband," Clarice said. "And the college, and finally, at an open meeting, the students."

"My God," Susan said.

"I had bared pretty much everything else to a con man. I guessed I could bare my soul to the people I loved," Clarice said.

"And they forgave you," Susan said.

"My husband said it was time to get help . . . for both of us. I agreed. I offered to resign from the college. They suggested instead that I take a leave of absence while my husband and I worked on things."

"And the students?" Susan said.

Clarice smiled with some warmth.

"I have found that girls of that age are both more and less judgmental than others," she said. "Some were astounded that a woman over forty could have an explicitly sexual affair. Some were titillated by it. A large number, I think, sort of shrugged and said, 'Yeah, yeah, you slept around. Doesn't everybody?' No one required me to wear a scarlet letter."

"How did Gary Astor take it?" I said.

"He was really very nice about it. When the detectives were taking him away, he grinned at me and said, 'For a good-looking broad, you got a lot of spine, Richie.' That's what he called me. He said Clarice was too European."

"And he did three in Shirley."

"Yes."

"Did you ever hear from him?" I said.

She flushed a little.

"His first year in prison he sent me flowers on my birthday," she said. "I never acknowledged them."

"Nothing since?"

"He wrote me a letter saying good-bye, that it had been fun while it lasted, that he'd always remember, ah, certain moments we'd had, and he wished me well."

"Anything else?" I said.

"No," she said. "He's a very pleasant man, I think. But he seems to have absolutely no moral or ethical sense. It's like someone with no sense of humor. There's nothing really to say about it, except that it isn't there."

"You ever miss him?" Susan said.

"I never want to see him again," Clarice said.

"And your marriage is stable?" Susan said.

"Eric and I spent two years in psychotherapy. Each with our own therapist. You remember Mr. Hemingway's remark?" she said.

"It heals stronger at the break," I said.

"You're a reader, Mr. Spenser?" she said.

"Susan helps me with the big words," I said.

Clarice smiled, with even more warmth in it.

"In retrospect, the entire incident was salvation for Eric and me. Each of us has come to terms with our demons. And we both had demons."

"A troubled marriage," Susan said, "nearly always has at least two."

"Has any of this been useful, Mr. Spenser?"

"It's been worth hearing," I said.

"But useful?"

"Gotta think about it," I said. "If any of my victims were willing, would you talk with them?"

She smiled again. This time with not only warmth but humor.

"The sisterhood is strong," she said.

"I'll take that," I said, "for a yes."

She nodded.

"You may," she said.

Chapter

❖

23

IT WAS MORNING, and we were in the car, drinking coffee, driving south on Route 91 heading for the Mass Pike. I was enjoying a donut.

"Sure you don't want one?" I said. "Cinnamon, my fave."

"Ick," Susan said.

"The naked frolic in a motel outside of Springfield seemed to go better than you thought it would," I said.

"A moment of weakness," Susan said.

"You think there's anything in the fact that what Clarice remembers best about her and Gary's sex life is how strong and forceful he was?"

"You think he might be a little vengeful?" Susan said.

"Something like that," I said. "I mean, even Hawk agrees that there's a limit to the number of women you can have sex with."

"And Hawk has tested the limits," Susan said.

"He has," I said. "You said once that there might be something more than sex and money in this deal."

"What could be more than sex and money?" Susan said.

"Pathology?" I said.

"Hey, I do the shrink stuff here," Susan said.

"And?"

"Might be," Susan said. "Worth looking into, I suppose."

"And how would I look into that?" I said.

"Talk to some of his other partners."

"Oh," I said.

I finished my donut and got another one out of the bag. Susan ate some grapes she'd brought with her from home.

"You think things really do heal stronger at the break?" I said.

"It's a nice metaphor," Susan said. "When a broken bone heals, there is often additional bone mass."

"So bones may in fact heal stronger at the break," I said.

"Maybe," Susan said.

"Think that holds in other things?" I said.

"Some things," she said. "Sometimes."

"There are very few absolutes in the therapist's canon," I said.

"Very few," Susan said. "Although, I guess, understanding the truth about yourself is important."

"You think they got there?"

"Clarice and her husband? Probably," Susan said. "No one gets there all the way. But they seem close. If she's accurate. I assume they addressed the causes of the break, understood them, and were tough enough to change."

"She was tough enough," I said, "not to knuckle under to Gary Eisenhower."

Susan smiled.

"You like that name, don't you?" Susan said.

"I do. If I adopt an alias, I may use it."

"Gee," Susan said. "You look just like a Gary Eisenhower, too."

"And from there it's an easy leap to Cary Grant," I said.

"Easy," Susan said. "Of course, guilt helped."

"Clarice?"

"Uh-huh."

"As in she was tough enough to confess publicly because she felt she deserved the public humiliation?" I said.

"As in exactly that," Susan said. "You're smarter than you look."

"Lucky thing," I said. "If I weren't, I probably wouldn't be able to feed myself."

"I'd feed you," Susan said.

"I know you would," I said. "But, guilt or whatever, it all worked for her. She kept her husband, her job, her children's regard."

"And her self," Susan said.

Occasionally as we drove we could see the Connecticut River flowing south beside us, heading for Long Island Sound. The year had gone too far into November for there to be much leaf color left. Here and there a yellow leaf, or none, or few, but mostly spare grayness, hinting of cold rain.

"So are you saying," I said, "that Gary's

current victims in the gang of four haven't got enough guilt?"

"A little guilt is not always a bad thing," Susan said.

"And you a psychotherapist," I said.

"I'm also Jewish," she said.

"I think that's a tautology," I said.

"Oy," Susan said.

"You think I should start berating them," I said. "Make them feel more guilty?"

"I don't know if it would work," Susan said. "But I suspect it's not your style."

We came to the pike and headed east. I had one of those toll transponders that allow you to zip through the fast lane unhesitatingly. It made me feel special.

"It is interesting, though, that none of them feels guilty enough for your scenario to work."

"It would suggest something about their marriages," Susan said.

"And about them," I said. "Some of them feel they'd be ruined if this all came out. One couple, the husband is gay, for instance, and in line for a big job. He and his wife are close. She knows, of course, and they remain friends, with a, necessarily, open marriage."

"You don't think that such fears beset Clarice Richardson?" Susan said.

"And they are not illegitimate fears," I said. "She was lucky to be in a situation where decency could prevail."

"That, too, would probably influence her," Susan said.

"The recognition of those circumstances, and the hope that decency would prevail," I said.

"Yes."

"Maybe I could get them to see you professionally, and you could berate them."

"Until they felt guilty enough to cure themselves?"

"Exactly," I said. "How would that fly at the Psychoanalytic Institute?"

"Banishment, I think," she said. "It is, however, not a position I'm prepared to take."

"Is there a position you are prepared to take?" I said.

Susan smiled her fallen-angel smile. One of my favorites.

"How about prone, big boy?" she said.

"Shall I stop on the roadside?" I said.

Susan smiled.

"No," she said.

Chapter

❖❖

24

WHEN GARY EISENHOWER came into my office on a rainy Monday morning, he had a purple bruise on his right cheekbone and a swollen upper lip. He moved stiffly to one of my chairs and eased himself into it. When he spoke he sounded like his teeth were clenched.

"I need a gun," he said.

"I would guess that you do," I said.

"I'm a convicted felon," he said. "I can't just buy one."

"Also true."

"Can you give me one?"

"Probably not," I said. "Who beat you up?"

He made a slight movement with his lips, which, if it hadn't hurt, might have turned into a smile.

"How'd you know?" he said.

"I'm a trained detective," I said.

"Couple guys came around, tole me to stay away from Beth Jackson."

"You're still seeing her?" I said.

"Yeah."

"Even though she hired me to put you out of business?" I said.

"Yeah," Gary said.

"She your mole in the gang of four?" I said.

"How'd you know there was a mole?"

"You knew who hired me," I said.

He shook his head and winced.

"And—" I said.

"You're a trained detective," Gary said.

"You tell them to take a hike?" I said.

"The two guys?" he said. "No, I said, 'Sure thing.'"

"But?"

He started to shrug and remembered that everything hurt and stopped in mid-shrug.

"But she kept coming around and"—again the try at a smile—"what's a boy to do?"

"So they caught you again and decided to get your attention," I said.

"Yeah."

"One of the guys slim and dark, sort of quiet?" I said.

"Yeah, Zel, he said his name was. The one poured it on me was some kind of ex-pug. He had a funny name, too, but I'm a little hazy about some of the details."

"Boo," I said.

"Yeah," Gary said. "Boo. He liked his work."

"So now what?" I said.

"I took my beating, but I'm not going away."

"So you'll see Beth again?"

"Absolutely."

"You care that much about her?"

"I like to fuck her," Gary said.

"She's not your only option," I said.

"I told you before, I'm tougher than I seem," Gary said. "I been punched around before. But I'll fuck who I want to fuck, and no one tells me who that can be."

"My God," I said, "a principled position."

"So I need a gun."

I shook my head.

"Can't give you a gun," I said. "But maybe I can take Zel and Boo off your back."

"You?"

"Yep."

"How you going to do that?" Gary said.

"Sweet reason," I said.

"'Sweet reason'?" Gary said. "You being funny?"

"I hope so," I said.

"How quick can you do this?"

"Pretty soon. In the meantime ask Beth to, ah, lay off, at least for a few days," I said.

"What are you going to do," Gary said.

"Talk to some people, arrange a few things, call in some favors," I said.

"Who you gonna talk to?" he said.

"I have friends in low places," I said. "Can you keep it in your pants for a few days while I save your life?"

Gary nodded.

"Why you doing this for me?" he said.

"Damned if I know," I said.

Chapter

❖

25

BETH IS STILL SEEING EISENHOWER," I said to Chet Jackson.

He sat across his desk from me, looking as hard-polished and expensive as he had last time.

"You think?" he said.

"It's why you sent Zel and Boo to see him," I said.

"They went to see him?" Chet said.

The view through the picture window behind him was still marvelous, but I'd seen it before. It was what I'd always thought about paying for a view. After a day or two you don't even notice it.

"Boo beat him up," I said.

"What a shame," Chet said.

"I don't want it to happen again," I said.

"And you think I've got something to do with it?"

I said, "Let's not screw around with this, Chet. I want you to call them off."

"And let that sonovabitch continue to bang my wife?" Chet said.

"That's a question to take up with the bangee," I said. "Not the banger."

The lines around Chet's mouth deepened. I could hear Susan's voice in my brain: *"Banger" and "bangee" are sexist distinctions,* the voice said, *implying aggression on the one side and passivity on the other.*

I know. I know. I can't think of everything. Then I heard her laugh.

"That's probably true," he said.

"But?"

"But I can't," he said.

I nodded.

"Because you love her," I said.

"Yes."

"Chet," I said. "This is not between you and Gary Eisenhower. This is between you and your wife. The problem won't be resolved by beating up Gary Eisenhower. It won't be resolved if you kill him."

"There'd be someone else," Chet said.

"Uh-huh."

"I know that," Chet said. "You think I don't know that? Hell, I even had some counseling about that."

"Uh-huh."

We were quiet. I could feel his resistance slide into place like a shield between us.

"I can't let the sonovabitch get away with it," Chet said.

"Even though you might do the same thing," I said.

"In his shoes? Sure," Chet said. "Might not get into blackmail, but the rest? Yeah, of course."

"So maybe you should back off with Boo," I said.

Chet shook his head.

"I gotta do something," he said.

"Will it help you with Beth?" I said.

He looked at me steadily for probably thirty seconds without speaking. Then he shook his head.

"I gotta do something," he said.

"Even if it doesn't take you where you want to go," I said.

"I'm a tough guy," he said. "But not that tough. I can't take it."

"Too bad," I said.

"You gonna do something?" Chet said.

"Yeah," I said.

"I may have to send Boo and Zel to see you."

"You may," I said.

We looked at each other. I felt sort of bad for him. But the shield was in place. The conversation was over. I stood and walked out.

Chapter

26

I CALLED HAWK on his cell phone.

"You with Eisenhower?" I said.

"I in the lobby of a motel in Waltham," Hawk said. "Gary upstairs, with a woman."

"First of the day?" I said.

"Uh-huh," Hawk said.

"Well, it's early still," I said.

"Uh-huh."

"He had anything to say since you been tagging along with him?"

"He want to know do I think I can handle Boo, if he shows up," Hawk said.

"And you said you could."

"But modestly."

"If it comes to that," I said. "Zel is the real issue."

"Shooter?"

"Yep."

"I never heard of him," Hawk said.

"Me, either, but if you meet him, you'll know."

"Like Vinnie," Hawk said.

"Or Chollo," I said.

"They do have the look," Hawk said.

"So does Zel."

"I keep it in mind," Hawk said.

"Anything else?"

"Eisenhower say he don't mind me tagging after him," Hawk said. "Long as I don't cramp his style."

"Are you cramping it?"

"Not so's I can tell," Hawk said. "Mostly I trying to learn from it."

"It's good to make the most of a learning opportunity," I said.

"He a pretty cool dude," Hawk said. "As you honkies go."

"He is," I said. "Maybe he's got some sort of natural rhythm."

"He ain't that cool," Hawk said. "But he

don't seem scared. He seem like he can handle getting beat up, ain't gonna change him."

"He claims he's tougher than he seems," I said.

"Might be," Hawk said.

"He ask you for a gun?" I said.

"Uh-huh," Hawk said.

"And?"

"I say why you need a gun, you got me."

"And he said?"

"I may not always have you."

"Which is true," I said.

"It is," Hawk said. "So I tell him you could retire your dick for a while, or at least use it someplace else."

"He didn't buy that," I said.

"Nope," Hawk answered. "Say he fuck who he wants when he wants and he ain't gonna change."

"Man of principle," I said.

"Sure," Hawk said. "People live by worse codes."

"And we know a lot of them," I said.

"Where you calling from?" Hawk said. "You sound kind of echo-y."

"Rowes Wharf," I said. "I'm looking at the water."

"You on you cell phone?" Hawk said.

"I am," I said.

"You dialed it by yo'self?" Hawk said.

"I did," I said.

"Man, you makin' progress," Hawk said.

"Susan's been helping me," I said.

Hawk's chuckle was very deep as he broke the connection.

Chapter

27

SUSAN AND I were in her booth in Rialto, where she always sat, because it was quiet and you could watch people come and go. We had just taken our first sip of our first drink when Hawk showed up with Gary Eisenhower.

"That's the best you could do for a date?" I said to Hawk.

"I just the babysitter," Hawk said. "You tole me to bring him."

Gary put out a hand to Susan and said, "Hi, I'm Gary."

Susan shook his hand.

"I'm Susan," she said.

Gary slid into the banquette next to Susan. Hawk took a chair on the outside next to me.

"So," Gary said. "This is the main squeeze?"

"Only," I said.

"Well," Gary said. "You going to limit yourself to one, this is a good one."

The waiter took their drink orders and went to get them.

"You are not yourself monogamous, Gary?" Susan said.

"You know I'm not," Gary said.

"I'd heard that," Susan said.

"Gets me in trouble sometimes," Gary said.

"I'd heard that, too," Susan said.

She looked at Hawk and at me.

She said, "I think you're pretty safe tonight, however."

"Yeah, are these guys the best? I mean the best."

"Yes," Susan said. "They are."

The waiter came to announce the specials. We listened and looked at the menu and ordered. We had a second round of drinks, except Susan. After that flurry of activity, Susan turned and smiled at Gary.

"I know it's none of my business," she said. "But I'll try not to let that inhibit me. Why are you so, ah, unmonogamous?"

"Unmonogamous," Gary said. "You got a way with words, huh?"

Susan waited.

"Unmonogamous." He laughed. "Well, I guess I'd answer why would I be unmonogamous. I mean, if you got a whole orchard full of peaches, why would you eat just one?"

Susan smiled and nodded.

"So," Gary said, "lemme turn it around? Why would I be monogamous?"

"I'm not necessarily arguing for monogamy," Susan said. "Just why in your case that nonmonogamy is so all-consuming."

"No, no," Gary said. "You didn't answer my question, you did one of those shrink tricks, turn it back to me. First you need to answer my question."

"Very astute of you," Susan said. "Did you know I was a shrink?"

"No."

"But you've had experience with shrinks."

"Enough to know bullshit when I hear it," he said. "No offense."

"None," Susan said.

"So. Why are you monogamous?" Gary said.

"Because unlike peaches, whose consumption is all there is—they taste good and that's the end of it—persons have a variety of meanings and dimensions, and surprises, and feelings. I like those things, too."

"And not sex?" Gary said. "You don't look like somebody would not like sex."

Susan smiled.

"Notice the *too*," she said.

"Oh, yeah," Gary said. "That's good, I was thinking, *What a waste*."

"Nothing is wasted," Susan said.

"Love to find out someday," Gary said.

Hawk glanced at me. I shook my head.

"Why?" Susan said.

"Why?" Gary said. "For crissake, look at you."

"Thanks, but that's it, I look good?"

"Of course."

"No other reason?" Susan said.

Gary looked at me and winked.

"Be fun to see the look on his face," he said, and tipped his head toward me.

"Not for me," Susan said.

"You love him," Gary said.

"I do," she said.

"*À chacun son goût,*" he said.

Chapter

·◆·

28

HAWK TOOK GARY home after dinner. Susan and I lingered in our booth while Susan had a cup of coffee and I didn't. A cup of coffee at night would keep me awake until after the summer solstice.

"I know you brought me to meet Gary and see what I thought," she said.

"And what do you think?" I said.

"Wow," Susan said.

"Wow what?" I said.

"A clinical wow," she said. "He's absolutely fascinating."

"In a clinical way," I said.

"Absolutely," she said. "He flirted with me the entire evening."

"I know."

"And he was very aware of you all the time," Susan said.

"I noticed that," I said.

"Sometimes you've been known to intervene," Susan said.

"Not this time," I said. "I'm kind of clinical myself."

"Well," Susan said. "He's no simple matter."

"You mean he's not just a womanizer?" I said. "Who's turned a hobby into a business?"

"Maybe he is," Susan said. "People aren't usually just one thing, though."

"So a new theory wouldn't necessarily replace the old one," I said.

Susan nodded and gave me a big smile.

"So you've been paying attention all these years," she said.

"I'm more than one thing, myself," I said.

"You certainly are," Susan said. "But think about Gary Eisenhower for a minute. What is his pattern?"

"Good-looking women with rich husbands," I said.

"And where did Clarice Richardson fit into that pattern?"

"She's good-looking," I said.

"And she had a husband," Susan said. "But not a rich one."

"Maybe he was still perfecting his craft," I said.

"Probably," Susan said. "But we've been looking at *rich*, when perhaps we should be looking at *husband*."

"You mean it matters to him that they're married?'

"And maybe it matters to him that he can cuckold the husbands."

"Which would explain why he flirted with you in front of me," I said.

"You're not exactly a husband, but you'd fill the role."

"And if that's what he's doing," I said, "how much more fun if he can extract money."

"Exactly," Susan said. "Particularly in these circumstances, when the money comes out of the husband's pocket. Whether the husband knows it or not."

"I'm not clear quite where Clarice fits in to this," I said.

"No," Susan said, "I'm not, either. There

are, of course, many men whose sexual fantasies are directed at successful women, or women in authority."

"Schoolteachers, doctors, lawyers." I grinned at her. "Shrinks."

"Yes."

"Take them down a peg," I said.

"Men like Gary often use sex to humiliate."

"Into which need the blackmail would also pay," I said.

"Yes. Plus, of course, the money is good as money."

"Sometimes a cigar is just a cigar?"

"Or sometimes it's a cigar as well as several other things," Susan said.

"You think the women are humiliated?" I said.

"Not necessarily," Susan said. "It may only be in his fantasy."

"You think all this is true of Gary?"

"I don't know," Susan said. "It's a theory of the case."

"Or several," I said. "But they're worth testing, I think."

"There's no reason to avoid the scientific method," Susan said.

I pretended to take notes on the palm of my hand.

"Whoops," Susan said. "I'm slipping into a lecture."

"But gracefully," I said.

Susan smiled.

"Anyway, it might pay off to go back over Gary's, ah, career, and see what patterns you can find, and see if they support our theory," she said.

"Your theory," I said.

"Okay. What is your theory?"

"That you may be right," I said.

"I will also make a small bet with you," Susan said.

"Which is?"

"He'll call me for a date," Susan said.

"No bet on that," I said. "But I'll bet you don't accept."

"I only date you, snookums," Susan said. "But if I were to go out with someone else, it wouldn't be Gary Eisenhower."

"Because?"

"I'm pretty sure it wouldn't be about me," Susan said.

"Is that an informed guess?" I said.

"It's a woman's-intuition guess," she said.

"Good as any," I said

She finished her coffee. I paid the check. Susan got her coat. And we left. On the stairs I put an arm around her shoulder. She looked up at me and smiled.

"'Snookums'?" I said.

"I'm the only one who knows," she said.

Chapter

❖

29

I MET BETH JACKSON for lunch in a restaurant in the Chestnut Hill Mall. She had a salad. In the spirit of the season I had a turkey sandwich.

"You're still seeing Gary Eisenhower," I said.

Beth was wearing a fur hat like a Russian Cossack, and she looked cuter than a body has a right to. She speared a cherry tomato from her salad and popped it into her mouth and chewed and swallowed.

"So?" she said.

"Didn't you hire me to get him out of your life?"

"That was then," she said. "This is now."

"What caused the change?" I said.

She ate a piece of lettuce and pushed her plate away. She blotted her lips with her napkin. Then she folded the napkin and put it down on the table. She took some lip gloss out of her purse and touched up her lips using a small makeup mirror. Then she put that away, put her purse on the floor beside her chair, and smiled at me.

"A girl's got a right to change her mind," she said.

"So now you don't want me to get him out of your life?" I said.

Her smile widened without becoming warmer. She put her hands together and touched the center of her upper lip with her steepled forefingers.

"I wanted you to get him out of everyone else's life," she said.

"So he could be all yours?" I said.

"Exactly," she said.

"He's blackmailing you," I said.

She shrugged.

"We need the money," she said.

"You and Gary?" I said.

"Yes," she said. "So we can be together. Chet can spare it."

"But why join the effort to get rid of him?" I said. "Why not just stay out of it, stay with him, and collect the money that the others are paying him."

"You think I'm the only one slipping back to him?"

"I've stopped trying to think," I said. "I'm just chasing information."

"I didn't want anyone to suspect that I was still with him," she said. "So I agreed to the deal with the lawyer and you. I figured I could help him, even, by being on the inside, you know?"

She was as perky as a chickadee but dumber.

"You keep seeing him," I said, "and you may get him killed."

"Killed? Who's going to kill him?"

I didn't answer. I wasn't sure why, but I wasn't ready to quite give Chet up yet.

She smiled.

"You think Chet would kill him? For me?"

I didn't answer that, either.

"That's kind of exciting," Beth said. "Isn't that kind of fun? Like an old-fashioned movie. You know? Men killing each other over me?"

"It's probably less fun than it looks," I said.

"Oh, poo," she said. "I can handle Chet."

"Maybe," I said. "But maybe Gary can't."

"So it is Chet?"

"Might be," I said.

Christmas carols were playing. Many people were carrying packages with Christmas wrapping. It was like being in a commercial. I looked at Beth. I could see the tip of her tongue as she ran it back and forth over her lower lip.

"Well, I'm not backing off," she said.

"Of course not," I said. "What's the most interesting thing about him?"

"Interesting?"

"Unusual, maybe," I said. "What's different about him?"

"That's easy. He is into it all the way."

"Is he more intense than other men?" I said.

"He is all over you. He gets hold of you, and you better like it, because if you don't, you're going to have to do it anyway, you know?"

"Forceful," I said.

She nodded.

"And you like forceful?" I said.

"Yeahhhh," she said.

She was breathing fast, now, as if she

had just run up stairs. And the tip of her tongue was running fast back and forth across her lower lip. When she spoke her voice sounded a little hoarse.

"You get off on this?" Beth said. "Talking about it?"

"Which do you like best?" I said. "Being with Gary or thinking that someone might try to kill him because of it?"

She put her steepled fingers to her mouth again and pressed and turned her head a little so that she was looking at me from the corners of her eyes.

"Both are nice," she said.

Chapter

30

MY FURTHER RESEARCH into Susan's theories of the case began the next morning. I called Abigail Larson and asked her if she could stop by my office. She seemed happy to be asked.

She arrived about four in the afternoon dressed to the nines and smelling of martini. She arranged herself in one of my client chairs and crossed her legs. Her skirt was short.

"I thought you were off the case," she said.

"Mostly because I have no case," I said.

"But I'm a nosy guy, and in my free time I still poke around at it."

"Well," she said.

"Can we talk about you and Gary a little?"

"Sure," she said. "But first, can a girl get a martini around here?"

"Absolutely," I said. "I'm a full-service gumshoe."

"Up," she said. "With olives."

I went to the little alcove where I had a refrigerator and a small cabinet, and made her a martini. I served it to her in a lowball glass.

"Sorry about the glass," I said. "I haven't gotten around yet to specialty glassware."

"Just so it contains alcohol," Abigail said.

I went back around my desk and sat. She drank some martini.

"God, that's good," she said. "I like a man that can make a good martini."

"Me, too," I said.

She didn't need a drink. She was drunk when she arrived. On the other hand, drunks are often talkative. The martini I gave her was big.

"Could I ask you some stuff about your sex life with Gary?"

"Well, aren't you quite the voyeur," she said.

She pronounced "quite" like "quit."

"It's an incidental benefit," I said. "Is there anything about Gary's behavior during sex that stands out in your memory."

"Hoo," she said. "You go right to it, don't you?"

"I do," I said.

"Turn you on to talk about it?" she said.

"I don't know," I said. "Let's talk about it and see."

"Men are weird," she said.

"You bet," I said. "What was there about him during sex that made him different, unusual, whatever?"

"Like was he big or not?" she said.

"Anything that seemed different from other men," I said.

"I had a lot other men, ya know," she said.

"I'm not surprised," I said. "How was Gary different."

She uncrossed her legs and slumped a little in the chair while she thought, or tried to. Her legs were straight out in front of her. The short skirt crept up her thighs a little higher.

"John . . . husband . . . just lays there, makes me do all the work, you know?"

"Sure," I said.

"Gary, he grabs hold of you . . ."

"And does the work?"

"Yes . . . no . . . holds me down, like . . ."

She stopped and looked at me blankly for a moment, then closed her eyes and began to slide slowly out of the chair. I got out around the desk in time to keep her off the floor, although her skirt was up around her waist. I got my arms around her under the arms, and got her up and sort of waltzed her slowly across my office toward the couch. She tried to kiss me as we went, and got the side of my mouth. I got her there and down onto the couch and straightened her legs, and pulled down her skirt.

Then I went back to my desk and got out a yellow pad and made a couple of notes. So far I had learned several things. Abigail Larson was a boozer. Her husband was not a sexual athlete. She bought lingerie at La Perla. None of which seemed very useful. But it was all I was going to get today. I couldn't think of anything else to do but sit with her until she woke up. Which eventually she did. But she didn't feel chatty. And I sent her home in a cab.

Chapter

·◆◆·

31

IN THE NEXT couple of days I talked with the rest of the gang of four and learned more than I ever wanted to know about having sex with Gary Eisenhower.

"It was like a rape fantasy sometimes," Nancy said.

"And you didn't mind?" I said.

"No," she said. "I've told you what I'm like."

"So you enjoyed the fantasy," I said.

She was silent a moment. Then, in a small voice, she said, "Yes."

Later I talked with Susan about it.

"None of that seems very enlightening," she said.

"Not to me. I was hoping it would to you."

Susan shook her head.

"About the rape fantasy thing?" I said.

"That was Nancy Sinclair?"

"Yeah."

"I suspect that tells us more about Nancy than it does about Gary," Susan said.

"Maybe he is just what he seems to be," I said.

"A happy-go-lucky cockhound?" Susan said.

"Yeah," I said. "Don't you ever come across somebody like that in your business?"

"People who are what they seem to be," Susan said, "generally don't seek psychotherapy."

"Good point," I said. "But as far as I can see, this is one of those instances when the cigar is just a cigar."

"Maybe you should talk to Clarice Richardson again," Susan said.

"Because she's smart enough to understand what she may have experienced," I said.

"Yes."

Susan was between patients. I was sitting in her office, across the desk from her. I was silent for a little while. I eyed the couch against the wall to my right.

"Anybody actually lie down on that thing?" I said.

"I believe you and I have," Susan said.

"I mean for therapy."

"You and I have," Susan said.

"Not that kind of therapy," I said.

"Yes," Susan said. "It is kind of a cliché, but some people find it very helpful."

I nodded. Neither of us spoke for a little while.

Then I said, "I can't do it by phone."

"No need," Susan said. "I'm sure she'll see you."

"Care for another trip to Hartland?" I said.

"No," Susan said.

"Two hours out, two hours back," I said.

"An easy day trip," Susan said.

"What about the naked frolic in the Hartland motel?"

"Nothing to stop you," Susan said.

"By myself?"

"Whatever floats your boat . . . snookums."

Chapter

❖

32

CLARICE RICHARDSON CAME around her desk and shook my hand when I entered her office.

"Come in," she said. "Sit down. I'm glad to see you."

I looked around.

"No campus cop this time," I said.

"You've charmed me into submission," she said.

"Happens all the time," I said.

"I assume you are still chasing Goran," she said.

"I'm trying to figure him out," I said.

Clarice smiled.

"You, too," she said.

"You mentioned when we talked last that when you were intimate, he seemed very strong."

"Yes," she said.

She smiled and looked away from me out at the now wintry landscape of her college.

"I attributed it to passion," she said.

"Susan suggested that it hints of sadism," I said.

"And she thought you should ask me about that?"

"She thinks you're the only one intelligent enough to understand your experience."

Clarice nodded.

"But not intelligent enough to have avoided it."

"Nobody gets out of here alive," I said.

She nodded.

"I didn't think of it at the time, but perhaps there was something . . . I'm not sure sadistic is exactly right . . . but vengeful, perhaps."

I nodded.

"Can you give me an example?" I said.

She blushed.

"I'm sorry," I said.

"I made this bed, so to speak. If I have to lie in it, I have to lie in it."

I might not have chosen that metaphor. But maybe if I felt guilty . . .

"He would say things," she said. "When he was . . . in me, he would say things like 'Got you now, don't I?'"

"Say it often?" I said.

"Things like that," she said.

"You think he had some animosity toward women?" I said.

"I never felt it," she said. "But in the circumstance, I was not at my most analytic, I fear."

"None of us is," I said. "Why do you suppose he had an affair with you?"

Clarice smiled.

"He found me attractive?" she said.

"Almost certainly," I said.

"And available," Clarice said.

"Were you wearing your wedding ring?" I said.

"I was," Clarice said.

"Even though you were, ah, trolling?"

"Maybe I was ambivalent," she said. "Maybe I didn't want to admit to myself I was trolling. Maybe I didn't want to look like an old maid."

"Fat chance," I said.

She smiled faintly.

"Thank you," she said.

"So he knew you were married," I said.

"But not to wealth," she said.

"Maybe the wealth was an afterthought."

She nodded.

"The thing is," Clarice said, "in an odd way, Eric and I owe this man a great deal. If I had not been with him, and if he had not tried to blackmail me, I don't think either Eric or I would have found the strength to get help with our problems . . . nor to solve them."

"But you did," I said.

"Yes."

I stood.

"I won't bother you again," I said.

And I left.

Chapter

❖

33

I TALKED WITH SUSAN on the phone for nearly an hour before we hung up. It was dark outside. My apartment was nearly still. There was a fire going, and the hiss of the logs supplied the only sound. I sat at my kitchen counter with a scotch and soda in a tall glass, with a lot of ice.

Was I involved in this thing because it resonated with me and Susan a long time ago? It had happened to me before. I didn't think I was, but I had learned enough to know that motivation, including my own, was often murky.

I sipped my scotch and looked at the fire.

One of my problems was trying to figure out which side I was on. I wasn't even sure how I wanted things to turn out. I had some sympathy for the women in the case, more for some than for others. I kind of liked Gary. The cuckolded husbands deserved some sympathy, but maybe some blame, or at least some of them.

I drank the rest of my scotch and made another drink.

I wasn't exactly sure what real crime had been committed. I didn't want Regina and Clifford Hartley's complicated but functioning marriage to be destroyed. I thought it would be a shame if Nancy went on through life thinking her sexuality was a sickness. Abigail was a drunk. Beth was . . . I didn't know what Beth was, but it wasn't good.

But there was something wrong with the whole setup. Everything kept turning out not to be quite what it started out seeming to be. There was a lot of bottled-up stuff lying around, and Boo and Zel were rattling around like loose ball bearings. So why did I care? One reason was that no one else had hired me to do anything, and I like to work. It might have had to do with me being stubborn.

I drank some scotch. It was clarifying. People always claimed it was a bad sign if you started drinking alone. I always thought to sit quietly and alone and drink a little now and then was valuable. Especially if you have a fire to look at. What was it Churchill said? "I have taken more from alcohol than alcohol has ever taken from me." Something like that. Good enough for Winnie, I thought, good enough for me.

I took my glass to my front window and looked down at Marlborough Street. The lights in the brick and brownstone buildings seemed very homey. Outside it was dark and cold. Inside was light and warmth. There were people living there together, some of them happily, some not.

Sometimes I thought that Susan was the only thing in life that I cared about. But I knew that if it were actually so, it would destroy us. We both needed to work. We had to do things. Making moon eyes at Susan was not a sufficient career. It was cases like the one I was on that reminded me now and then that I could care about other things.

There was more sex in this case than I'd seen in a while, but none of it seemed connected to love. I realized as I looked out my window at the still city street that one of the things I was looking for in this mess was something grounded in love. Maybe the Hartleys, in their odd and bearded marriage, might be driven by love. Maybe not. Clarice Richardson's reformation and triumph might have been grounded in love. But it could have been grounded in guilt, and survival . . . and courage.

"Good for you, Clarice," I said. "Either way."

As I drank my final scotch, I decided that I had two things to do next. One, I had to defuse Chet Jackson, and second, I had to find out a little more about Gary Eisenhower, aka Goran Pappas. Having a plan made me feel decisive, or maybe it was the three scotches.

I washed my empty glass and put it away. I put a steak on the kitchen grill. In a sauté pan, I cooked onions, peppers, mushrooms, and a handful of frozen corn with olive oil, rosemary, and a splash of sherry. I had some herbed biscuits left

from Sunday when Susan and I had breakfast. I warmed them in the oven and when
everything was ready, I ate.

And drank some beer.

Chapter

........................◆◆........................

34

THE FIRST TWO PEOPLE I saw when I went into Buddy Fox's were Ty-Bop and Junior. Ty-Bop was a skinny kid, strung out on something. He did the gun work. Junior was the size of Des Moines but meaner. He did the muscle work.

"Junior," I said. "How's it going with Weight Watchers?"

"You looking to see Tony?" Junior said.

Ty-Bop stared at me as he jittered against the back wall of the restaurant, listening to his iPod. He showed no sign of recognition, although he'd seen me probably a hundred times. His eyes were empty.

His face was empty. He shot at what Tony told him to shoot at and, as best as I could tell, had no other interests except controlled substances and whatever music he was listening to. I don't think I'd ever heard him speak. But he could shoot. He might have been as good as Vinnie, maybe even Chollo, who was the best I'd ever seen.

"Wait here," Junior said.

He went past the bar and down a hall. Ty-Bop looked at me blankly. I grinned at him.

"How are things, Ty-Bop?" I said.

He jived a little and his head might have moved, but it was probably to the music.

"Listening to a different drummer?" I said.

Ty-Bop's expression didn't change.

"Good," I said. "I like an upbeat approach."

The room showed little sign that the South End had undergone considerable social change in the last twenty years. I was still the only white face in the room. Junior returned and jerked his head at me. I gave Ty-Bop a friendly thumbs-up and followed Junior past the bar. He was so big he could barely fit into the hallway, and both of us were too much. He stepped aside and gestured for me to walk past him.

"You know the door," he said.

"Like my own," I said, and walked on down the hall.

Tony's office was small and without much in the way of ostentation. Tony was in there with Arnold, who was his driver. Arnold didn't shoot as well as Ty-Bop or muscle as well as Junior. But he was a nice combination of both skills, and he had a little class. He was handsome as hell. And dressed great.

"Arnold," I said.

"Spenser."

Arnold was sitting on a straight chair, turned around so he could rest his forearms on the chair back. Tony was behind his desk. A little soft around the neck and jawline. But very dignified-looking, with a scatter of gray in his short hair, and none in his carefully trimmed mustache. As always, he was dressed up. Dark suit, white shirt, maroon silk tie and pocket hankie. He was smoking a long, thin cigar.

"Tony," I said. "Do you color your mustache?"

Tony Marcus smiled.

"Actually, motherfucker," he said, "I color my whole body. In real life, I'm a honkie."

"Nope," I said. "No white guy can say 'motherfucker' like you do."

Tony nodded.

"Whaddya want?" he said.

"Need a favor," I said.

"Oh, good," Tony said. "Been hoping some wiseass snow cone would come in and ask for a favor."

"You want me to pat him down?" Arnold said to Tony.

"No need," Tony said.

"He's got a gun," Arnold said. "I can tell the way his coat hangs."

Tony looked at Arnold.

"You done work with him, you think we need to worry 'bout the gun?"

"No."

"Okay," Tony said, and turned to me, and raised his eyebrows.

"Know a guy named Chet Jackson?" I said.

"Who wants to know?" Tony said.

"That would be me," I said. "I look like some kind of bicycle messenger?"

"Why do you want to know?"

"He's a danger to someone I sort of represent," I said.

"And you can't stop him?"

"Not without killing somebody," I said.

"So?" Tony said.

"Not my style," I said.

"So have Hawk do it for you," Tony said.

"Also not my style."

"But it your style to come ask me," Tony said. "A simple African-American trying to get along in a flounder-belly world?"

"Exactly," I said.

Tony smiled.

"I know Chet Jackson," he said.

"You have any clout with him?"

"I might," Tony said. "Pretty much got clout wherever I need it."

"So much for the simple African-American," I said.

Tony smiled again.

"You knew that was bullshit when you heard it," he said. "I don't know if I owe you anything or not. But you done me some favors."

"Cast your bread upon the waters," I said.

"Sure," Tony said. "Tell me a story."

I told him as much as he needed to know.

Tony listened without interrupting while he smoked his cigar. When I was done, he put the cigar out in a big glass ashtray on his desk and leaned back in his chair.

"What the fuck," he said, "are you doing mixed up in crap like that?"

"I ask myself that from time to time," I said. "But I'm a romantic, Tony. You know that."

"Whatever that means," he said.

We sat. Tony got out a new cigar and trimmed it and lit it, and got it going evenly, turning the cigar barrel slowly in the flame of Arnold's lighter.

"So how you want to do this?" he said.

Chapter

35

ACCORDING TO his police folder, Goran Pappas had graduated in the top quarter of his Richdale High School class and gone on to Wickton College on a basketball scholarship.

Wickton was a small liberal-arts college just across the New Hampshire line, south of Jaffrey. I spent the next day there and worked my way slowly through a host of reticent academics to arrive late in the day in the office of the director of counseling services. According to the plaque on her desk, her name was Mary Brown, Ph.D.

"Dr. Brown," I said. "My name is Spenser.

I'm a detective. I've been wandering your campus all day and am in desperate need of counseling."

She was a sturdy woman with gray hair and rimless glasses.

"I can see why you would," she said. "Please sit down."

I did.

"I'm trying to learn about a man who attended this college. Everyone who would know agrees he did. But no one will tell me much about him."

"Because they don't know much?" she said.

"Because they don't know, or think it's confidential, or don't like detectives."

"Surely that couldn't be it," she said.

"I was being self-effacing," I said.

"I have been here for more than thirty years," she said. "Perhaps I can help. What is the man's name?"

"Goran Pappas," I said.

She was quiet for a moment. The rimless glasses were strong, and they seemed to enlarge her eyes as she looked at me through them.

"I remember him," she said.

"What can you tell me?" I said.

She smiled.

"What can you tell *me*?" she said.

"About anything you want to know," I said.

"Then do so," she said.

I told her everything I thought she'd want to hear, omitting only the names, except for Goran. When I was through she sat for a time, frowning.

"My goodness," she said. "And what is it you are trying to accomplish?"

"To right the unrightable wrong, I suppose," I said.

"I understand the allusion," she said. "But specifically, what do you hope to accomplish?"

"I feel a little silly saying it. But . . . right now everything is coming out badly for pretty much everyone involved, except maybe the college president. . . . I'd like to make everything come out okay."

She looked at me silently through the distorting rimless lenses for a time and then reached up and tilted them lower on her nose and looked over them at me.

"My God," she said.

I shrugged and gave her my sheepish smile. She seemed stable enough to risk the sheepish smile. Less stable women were known to undress when I did the sheepish smile. I was right. She remained calm.

"How can I check on you?" she said.

"If I could borrow a sheet of paper," I said.

She gave me one. And I wrote down the names and phone numbers and recited them as I wrote.

"Captain Healy, homicide commander, Mass state cops," I said. "Martin Quirk, homicide commander, Boston police. FBI man named Epstein, AIC in Boston."

"AIC?"

"Agent-in-charge," I said. "And Susan Silverman, Ph.D., who's a psychotherapist in Cambridge."

I handed her the paper.

"In the interest of full disclosure," I said. "Dr. Silverman is my honey bun."

"'Honey bun,'" Mary said.

"Girl of my dreams," I said.

"I'll get back to you, Mr. Spenser," Mary said.

Chapter

36

I WASN'T SURE WHO HAD TOLD what lies to accomplish it. But we were all assembled when Hawk brought Gary Eisenhower into Chet Jackson's office. Chet was at his desk. Tony was in a chair across from Chet, with Junior and Ty-Bop leaning against the wall in the back of the room; Beth sat on the couch near him. Zel and Boo leaned on the wall near Chet, looking at Junior and Ty-Bop. I stood near the door.

When he got inside the room, Gary paused and looked around.

"Hot damn," he said, and walked across the room and sat beside Beth on the couch.

"'S happening, Beth?" he said, and patted her on the thigh.

She smiled brightly.

"Okay," Chet said. "You put this together, Tony. Talk to us."

Tony looked around the office.

"Lotta firepower in here," he said.

Chet nodded.

"Hawk," Tony said. "Spenser. My friends, your goons. Lotta force."

I could tell that Boo felt dissed by being called a goon. But he didn't speak. Zel seemed uninterested.

"So?" Chet said.

"I hope there's no need for force," Tony said.

"To do what?" Chet said.

"To resolve our problem."

"Our problem? What problem do you and me have?" Chet said.

Tony looked around the room. He took out a cigar, trimmed it, lit it, got it going, took in some smoke, and exhaled.

"We don't have to get too explicit here," he said. "But you and I do business in the same territory, and we got an agreement in place that allows us to do that without, you know, rubbing up against each other."

Chet nodded without saying anything.

"That gonna end," Tony said, "'less you straighten out your love life."

"My love life," Chet said.

Tony took an inhale on his cigar and took it from his mouth, held it up in front of him, and exhaled so that he looked at the glowing end of the cigar through the smoke.

"Specifically, Mr., ah, Eisenhower," Tony said. "I want him left alone."

"What the hell do you care?" Chet said.

"Don't matter why," Tony said. "Only matter that I do."

"And if I tell you to go to hell?" Chet said.

"You're out of business," Tony said.

Everyone was quiet. Beth looked bright-eyed and excited as she watched the back-and-forth between her husband and Tony Marcus. Gary Eisenhower looked sort of amused, but he nearly always looked amused. Maybe because he was always amused. The damned cigar kept being a cigar.

"You think you can put me out of business?" Chet said.

"I know I can," Tony said. "And so do you."

Chet nodded slowly.

"You and Spenser rig this deal?" Chet said.

"Don't matter who rigged it," Tony said. "It rigged. Take it or leave it."

"He a friend of yours?" Chet said.

I knew he was stalling while he tried to think it through.

"He sent me up once," Tony said. "So no, we ain't friends. But he done me some favors, too."

Everyone was quiet.

Then Boo said, "Mr. Jackson, you want me to take one of these clowns apart, you just say so."

Tony turned and looked at him with mild amusement. Zel shook his head sadly and stepped away from Boo, his gaze fixed on Ty-Bop, who was still nodding to whatever music he was hearing in the spheres, but he was as focused on Zel, and Zel was on him.

"Boo took too many to the head," Zel said, "when he was fighting."

"Screw you, Zel," Boo said. "We ain't hired to let people push our boss around."

Beth's eyes seemed even brighter, and I noticed her tongue moving along her lower lip again. Tony was incredulous.

"You think you gonna take Junior apart?" Tony said, tilting his head in Junior's direction. It was an easy tilt, because Junior occupied most of the room.

"Anybody in the room," Boo said.

His eyes still steady on Ty-Bop, Zel shook his head sadly.

"Boo," he said softly.

"You heard me," Boo said.

Behind his desk, Chet looked blankly at the scene. He very likely had no idea what he was supposed to do.

Boo was staring at Junior.

"How 'bout you, boy? You want to try me?"

Junior looked at Tony. Tony nodded. Junior smiled.

I said, "How 'bout me, Boo?"

And he turned toward me.

"You, wiseass?" he said. "Be a pleasure."

I slipped out of my jacket. Boo came at me in his fighter's stance. He threw a left hook to start, and I saw right away why his face was so marked up. He dropped his hands when he punched. I blocked his hook with my right and put a hard jab onto his nose. It didn't faze him. He kept coming. He faked a left and tried an overhand right.

I took it on my forearm and nailed him with a right cross, and he went down. He got right back up, but his eyes were a little unfocused, and his hands were at his waist. I hit him with my right forearm and then torqued back and hit him with the side of my right fist. He went down again. He tried to get up and made it to his knees, and wobbled there on all fours. Zel squatted beside him.

"Nine, ten, and out," he said to Boo. "Fight's over."

Boo stayed where he was, his head hanging. Some stubborn vestige of pride that he wouldn't let go and be flat on the floor. Zel stayed with him.

"Come on, big guy," Zel said. "Let's get out of here."

Boo made a faint gesture with his head that was probably an affirmative, and Zel got an arm around him and helped him up. Boo was more out than in, but his feet moved.

As they passed, Zel said to me, "Thanks."

I nodded.

And they went out.

"So much for your muscle," Tony said.

Chet nodded.

"I thought he was tougher than that," Chet said.

"He was," I said.

"Probably been beating up loan-shark deadbeats too much," Gary said, and grinned. "Or guys like me."

Beth was staring at me silently. Her face was a little flushed. Her tongue was still on her lower lip, but it wasn't moving.

"What about it, Chet?" Tony said.

Chet looked at me and back at Tony. Then he looked at Beth.

"Okay," he said. "I lay off Gary Boy."

"Right choice," Tony said.

"But"—Chet turned to Beth—"it stops here. I am not going to be your patsy."

"Meaning?" Beth said.

"You drop Gary Boy here, or I'll throw you out without a dime."

"You'd divorce me?"

"I would."

She looked at Gary.

"You got no case," Gary said. "He wouldn't have to give you anything."

"And if I give him up?" she said to Chet.

"And keep your knees together," Chet said. "We walk into the sunset together."

"That's my choice?"

Chet looked at her as if they were alone in the room.

"I love you," Chet said. "But I can't be out of business. If I was, you'd leave me anyway, soon as the money ran out."

"You think that of me?" Beth said.

"I know it of you," Chet said. "But it's okay. I knew it when I married you. I made the deal. I'll live with it. But I'm not giving up both you and the money."

Beth looked at Tony Marcus.

"This man can actually put you out of business?" she said.

"Yes," he said. "He can."

Beth looked at Gary.

"What should I do?"

"I was you," Gary said, "I'd dump me and go for the dough."

Beth nodded.

"Okay," she said.

Tony grinned and stood up.

"Our work here is done," he said.

Chapter

❖

37

NOW THAT HE didn't have to babysit Gary Eisenhower anymore, Hawk was at leisure, so he rode up to Wickton College with me.

"So how come you didn't let Boo have a go at Junior?" he said.

"Junior would have killed him," I said.

"So?"

"No need for it," I said.

Hawk shrugged.

"And how come we going up to talk to these people 'bout Gary Eisenhower? Ain't that all wrapped up?"

"Told her I would," I said.

"Who?"

"Director of counseling at the college," I said.

We were on Route 2, west of Fitchburg. Mostly bare winter trees to look at.

"You a bear for cleaning up loose ends," Hawk said.

"I'm a curious guy," I said.

"You sho' nuff are," Hawk said.

We turned off Route 2 and headed north on 202 toward Winchendon. We stopped for coffee, and in another half-hour we were at Wickton College.

"Don't see a lot of African-Americans 'round here," Hawk said.

"You may be the first," I said.

"At least I the perfect specimen."

"You want to come in with me, Specimen?" I said.

"Naw," Hawk said. "I think I sit here and see if I attract the attention of some college girls."

"I don't want to discourage you," I said. "But no one paid any attention to me when I was here last time."

Hawk looked at me silently for a while.

Then he said, "What that got to do with me?"

I left him and went in to see Mary Brown.

"Your recommendations support you," she said when I was seated. "Particularly your honey bun."

"Good to know," I said.

"I obviously cannot break confidence with Mr. Pappas," she said. "But I can tell you things that are on the public record."

I waited.

"Our campus security officers do not have full police powers, so if there's an incident we ask the local police to step in," she said.

I waited some more.

"Mr. Pappas had a penchant for women who were with other men," she said. "This precipitated several fights. Often with alcohol involved. On one occasion our security officers had to call local authorities to stabilize the situation."

"And Mr. Pappas got busted?" I said.

"Yes."

"And booked?" I said.

"Yes."

"So if I were to speak to the local cops, I might learn something."

"Yes."

"Do you know what I might learn?" I said.

"I believe so," she said.

"I don't wish to compromise your ethics," I said. "But if I'm going to know it anyway, why not save me a trip to the fuzz."

She thought about that for a time.

"He was released without penalty under the condition that he seek counseling from a psychotherapist."

"There's one around here?"

"One," she said. "He has offices in the medical center."

"Name?" I said.

She hesitated.

"His name is Paul Doucette," she said. "I've alerted him that you might visit."

"Hot damn," I said. "So you were going to tell me this before I even arrived."

"I thought I might," she said.

"So it wasn't my clever questioning," I said.

"No."

"How about charm," I said.

"Well," she said, and smiled. "That was certainly part of it."

"Oh, good," I said. "Is it enough to get me directions, too?"

"We have them preprinted," she said, and took a card out of a file on her desk and handed it to me.

"Thank you," I said.

"Your honey bun was very persuasive," Mary said.

When I came out of the administration building, Hawk was leaning on the fender, talking with two college girls.

"This is Janice, and Loretta," Hawk said. "We been discussing African tribal practices."

"Any particular tribe?" I said.

"Mine," Hawk said.

The girls said, "How do you do."

"Have to excuse us," I said. "Gotta go down to the medical center."

"He scared to go alone," Hawk said.

The girls said good-bye, we got in, and the girls waved after us as we drove away.

"What tribe was that again?" I said.

"I forgot," Hawk said.

Chapter

◆◆◆

38

THE MEDICAL CENTER was a two-story brick building with a lot of glass windows, and a parking lot beside it. When I parked, Hawk got out with me.

"You going to hang around out here?" I said to Hawk. "And further integrate the region?"

"Must be nurses here," Hawk said, and resumed residence on my front fender.

I went in to talk to Dr. Doucette. It took a while, but he squeezed me in between patients. He was a lean, fiftyish man with silvery hair combed straight back. He looked like he might play racquetball.

I gave him my card.

"Mary Brown called me, so I know who you are," he said. "I'm Paul Doucette. I haven't much time, and there are obviously issues of confidentiality. That given, how can I help you?"

"Tell me what you can about Goran Pappas," I said.

"I interviewed him and found him a reasonably coherent young man with a passion for women, particularly women already with another man."

"Any reason for that?"

"The interest in other men's women?" Dr. Doucette said. "Probably, but it didn't seem to consume him. He seemed perfectly able to control it if he chose to. His life didn't make him unhappy, and he appeared to present no particular threat to society."

"So you had nothing much to treat him for," I said.

"Correct. I told the police and the college that in my opinion, he was well within the normal range of appropriate behavior."

"Did you explore the other-men's-women business with him?"

"I did."

"Can you tell me about it?"

"No."

"Would I be revealing my ignorance," I said, "if I suggested that if I were looking into it, I'd start with his mother and father."

"In my business," Doucette said, "as perhaps in yours, it is sensible to start with the most obvious and see where it leads."

"Can you tell me where it led you?"

"No," he said. "I can't. But perhaps you can tell me why you want to know."

I smiled.

"Just because I don't know, I guess."

"Has Pappas committed a crime?"

"Well, sort of."

"'Sort of'?" Doucette said.

I told him a brief outline of the Gary Eisenhower story.

Doucette nodded.

"So," he said. "I gather that from your perspective, though he won't be punished for the blackmail, the case is resolved."

"Yes."

He looked at his watch.

"And you'll settle for that," he said.

"Yes."

"For what it's worth," he said. "I agree with you."

"It's not perfect," I said.

"It never is," Doucette said.

"But I'll take it," I said.

"I do not believe Pappas is a bad man," Doucette said. "He is, by and large, what he appears to be."

"So you'll take it, too," I said.

"I did," Doucette said.

He looked at his watch again. I nodded and stood. We shook hands. And I headed out to the parking lot to see how many nurses Hawk had wrangled.

Chapter

39

I HAD A DRINK with Gary Eisenhower at the bar in a new steakhouse called Mooo, up near the State House.

"I got this one," he said when I sat down beside him. "I guess I owe you that much."

"Probably more than that," I said.

"You think?"

He had a Maker's Mark on the rocks. I ordered beer.

"I took Jackson and his people off your back," I said.

"Pretty clever how you did that," Gary said. "You know some scary dudes."

"I do," I said.

"You're pretty scary yourself," Gary said.

With his forefinger he stirred the ice in his bourbon.

"I know," I said.

"How come you fought Boo?" Gary said.

"Junior would have killed him," I said.

"The huge black dude is named Junior?" Gary said.

"Yep."

"Man," Gary said. "I'd hate to see Senior."

I nodded.

"Why do you care if Junior kills Boo?" Gary said.

"No need for it," I said.

"Boo's not much," Gary said. "Except mean."

"I know."

"Why would he go with the biggest guy in the room?"

"It's all he's got," I said. "He's a tough guy. He doesn't have that, he has nothing. He isn't anybody."

"And you took that away from him," Gary said.

"I did," I said. "But he's alive. And in a few days he'll beat up some car salesman who's fallen behind on the vig, and his sense of self will be restored."

"That easy?" Gary said.

"Boo's not very smart," I said.

"I'll say."

Gary ordered another bourbon. I ordered another beer.

"Zel was, like, looking out for him," Gary said.

"Yeah."

"I don't know this game like you do," Gary said. "But I saw Zel move a little away from Boo when the trouble started, and focus in on the skinny black kid."

"Ty-Bop," I said.

"And I figure if things went bad for Boo," Gary said, "Zel would start shooting."

"Unless Ty-Bop beat him," I said.

"Either way," Gary said. "We weren't far from a shoot-out right there."

"True."

"In which several people might have got killed," he said.

"True."

"Including Beth," he said.

"Including Beth."

"You thinking about that," Gary said, "when you stepped up?"

"Sure," I said.

"Christ," Gary said. "A fucking hero."

"But you knew that anyway," I said.

Gary laughed and sipped some bourbon.

"So," I said. "I think you owe me more than two beers."

"How many?" Gary said.

"I think you need to stop blackmailing these women," I said.

"Ones that hired you?"

"Yep."

"You get some kind of bonus?" he said.

"Nope."

"You got a bonus, maybe we could split it."

"Stop blackmailing these women," I said.

"What if I fuck them for free?" Gary said.

"That's between you and them," I said. "But no blackmail."

"And I pick up this tab?" Gary said.

"Nope," I said. "I'll get the tab.

Gary grinned and put out his hand.

"Deal," he said.

And we shook on it.

Chapter

40

IT WAS DECEMBER NOW. Gray, cold, low clouds, snow expected in the afternoon. I was in my office, drinking coffee and writing out my report on a missing child I'd located. My door opened without a knock, and Chet Jackson came in wearing a double-breasted camel-hair overcoat.

"The mountain comes to Mohammed," I said.

"Whatever," Chet said. "Mind if I sit down?"

I said I didn't, and he unbuttoned his overcoat and sat without taking it off.

"I want you to keep an eye on my wife," he said.

"To what purpose?"

"You know to what purpose," Chet said. "I want to make sure she's faithful."

"Eisenhower?" I said.

"That's one worry," he said.

"Hard to tail someone who knows you," I said.

"That's fine," he said. "If she spots you, she won't do it."

"Because she knows I'll report it to you," I said.

"Yes."

"And you'll divorce her and cut her off without a penny."

"Yes," he said. "I will."

"So I provide both information and a certain degree of prevention," I said.

"Exactly," he said.

"How long would you plan to keep track of her like this?" I said.

Chet looked startled.

"I . . . there's no timetable," he said. "We'll play it by ear."

I tilted my chair back and put a foot up on my desk.

"You want her to be faithful, but you don't trust her, and you're trying to compel her," I said.

"I love her," he said.

"And she loves you?"

"She's been with me for ten years," he said. "The sex is still good."

"You ever read Machiavelli?" I said.

"I imagine somebody mentioned him to me at Harvard."

"He argued that it is better to be feared than loved," I said. "Because you can make someone fear you, but you can't make them love you."

"I'll settle for what I can get," Chet said.

"I understand that," I said. "But I'm not your man."

I thought I saw a glitter of panic in Chet's eyes.

"Why not?"

"Couple of things," I said. "One, I'm sick of all of you. All the women and their husbands and the whole cheating rigmarole. Two, it's emotional suicide. And I'm not going to help you commit it."

"What are you, some kind of fucking shrink?"

"Doesn't matter what I am," I said. "I'm not going to work for you."

"What if I pay you more than you're worth?" Chet said.

"There is no such amount," I said. "But it's not about money. I won't dance."

Chet was rich. He had clout. People didn't turn him down. He was breathing as if he had just run a race. His wife didn't love him, and he didn't think he could live without her.

"I need some help here," he said.

His voice was hoarse.

"You do," I said. "But not the kind I can give you."

"You talking about a shrink?" he said.

"I can get you some names," I said.

"Fuck that," he said.

I didn't say anything.

"Fuck that," he said again, and got up and walked out.

Outside my office window, a couple of solitary snowflakes spiraled down. I watched them as they passed.

"Après vous," I said, "le déluge."

Chapter

❖❖

41

NORMALLY WHEN WE ATE TOGETHER at my place, Susan and I sat at the kitchen counter. But it was Christmas, so Susan set the table at one end of the living room: table-cloth, crystal, good china, good silver, candles, and napkins in gold napkin rings.

"What do you think?" Susan said.

"Zowie," I said.

"Zowie?"

"You heard me," I said.

"Would Martha Stewart say 'zowie'?"

"If she wouldn't, she should," I said.

I had a fire going, and Pearl the Wonder Dog was in front of it on the couch, resting up after the rigors of the ride from Cambridge.

"What's for eats?" Susan said.

"I was thinking pizza," I said. "How 'bout you?"

Susan looked at me without expression.

"Or Chinese?" I said. "I bet PF Chang's is open. Pork fried rice?"

Susan's expression didn't change.

"I suppose subs wouldn't do it, either," I said.

"The baby and I are going home," Susan said.

"Boy, are you picky," I said. "Okay, how about we start with bay scallops seviche, then we have slow-roasted duck, snow peas, corn pudding, and brown rice cooked with cranberries?"

"And dessert?" Susan said.

"Blackberry pie."

"With ice cream?" Susan said.

"Ice cream or cheddar cheese that I bought at Formaggio."

"Or both?"

"Or both," I said.

"Oh, all right," Susan said. "We'll stay."

"Good girls," I said. "Would either of you care for some pink champagne?"

"Pearl's underage," Susan said.

"In dog years she's middle-aged," I said.

"She is still a baby," Susan said.

"Okay," I said. "I'll drink hers. How about you, little lady?"

Susan smiled, which was worth traveling great distances to see, and said, "It would be foolish not to."

I poured us each a glass of Krug rosé, put the ice bucket on the coffee table, and Susan and I squeezed onto the couch beside Pearl. Pearl looked a little annoyed, which was hardly in the spirit of the season, but she readjusted her position and went back to sleep with her head on Susan's lap. Which was what I had been planning on.

"So," I said. "Do Jews go to hell for celebrating Christmas?"

"Jews don't go to hell," Susan said.

"None?"

"And in particular," Susan said, "none who were cheerleaders at Swampscott High."

"And still retain their skills," I said.

"Several skills," Susan said.

"I know."

We drank our champagne. The fire enriched itself as the logs settled in on one another. Pearl sighed in her sleep.

"Do we love each other?" Susan said.

"We do," I said.

"And were you thinking of celebrating that love with some sort of holiday rendezvous?"

"I was," I said.

"If I have a heavy meal, as I expect to," Susan said, "my libido will be dysfunctional for hours."

"I've noticed that about you," I said.

"However, if we were to drink a bit more champagne and retire to your bedroom before dinner, we could celebrate Christmas in our own ecumenical way," Susan said. "And then eat the big meal."

"Brilliant," I said. "You're amazing."

"Hot, too," she said.

I nodded.

"Hotter than a pepper sprout," I said.

"So shall we do that?"

"You bet," I said.

"Okay, pour me another glass of champagne," Susan said. "And we'll proceed."

"Zowie," I said.

Chapter

❖❖

42

IT WAS THE WEEK before Valentine's Day, and I was in my office working on the first draft of my Valentine's poem to Susan, when Gary Eisenhower arrived with Estelle, the trainer and putative girlfriend. I put the draft in my middle drawer.

"Gary," I said.

"Spenser," Gary said. "You remember Estelle?"

"I do," I said. "How are you, Estelle."

"Feeling good," she said, and gave me a big smile.

Gary gave her a hug.

"Main squeeze," he said, and kissed her on top of the head.

"Amazing that you find the time," I said.

"We manage," Estelle said.

I gestured toward the chairs and they sat down.

"We need to consult you," Gary said.

"Go," I said.

"It's about Beth Jackson," Estelle said.

"She seeing you again?" I said to Eisenhower.

"Not really," he said. "Her husband's all over her on that one. But she does see Estelle."

"I'm her trainer," Estelle said. "And we've become good friends."

"Still at Pinnacle?" I said.

"Yes, four days a week," Estelle said. "We do weights twice a week and Pilates twice a week."

"Estelle has been able to sneak me in a couple of times, and I've been able to spend a little time with Beth in one of the massage rooms."

"How modern of you," I said to Estelle.

She smiled brightly.

"Gary and I have our priorities straight," she said. "We know what we want."

"Which includes money," I said.

"Of course," Estelle said. "No point writing anyone off too soon."

"How's business?" I said to Gary.

Gary waffled his hand.

"Mezzo mezz," he said. "I'm just doing Beth to be polite. No income there at the moment. Meanwhile, I'm developing a new client list, but it's a little lean right now."

"Did you come to borrow money?" I said.

"No," Estelle said. "It's about Beth. I'm not only her trainer, I'm her friend."

"Friends are good," I said.

"There's someone threatening her life," Estelle said.

"Who?"

"She doesn't know. It's someone Chet does business with. He has threatened to kill Chet and Beth."

"Cops?" I said.

"Chet refuses to go to the police. Says it's nothing. Says he'll take care of it."

I nodded.

"Will you talk with her?" Estelle said.

I looked at Gary.

"You think it's serious?" I said.

"You know me, buddy," Gary said. "I don't think anything is serious."

"She's terrified," Estelle said. "She wants you to help her. But she's afraid to ask you."

I took in a long, slow breath.

"She thinks you're terrific," Estelle said. "You're the only one she thinks she can trust."

"She's probably right on both counts," I said. "When can she come in?"

"I'll bring her in tomorrow," Estelle said. "At five."

"Swell," I said.

Chapter

❖

43

BETH PUT A NOTE on my desk when she came in.

"Read this," she said.

**Your husband had betrayed me.
For this you both shall die.**

"Your husband has seen this?"

"Yes. He said it was a hoax and not to worry."

"But you are worried."

"I'm terrified. For both of us. Who would send such a thing?"

"I'll talk with him," I said.

"I promised my husband I would say nothing to anyone," Beth said.

"Except Estelle," I said. "And Gary. And me."

Estelle sat beside Beth across the desk from me and said nothing. The loyal, self-effacing friend.

"I'm frightened," Beth said. "I have to confide in someone. Estelle and Gary both urged me to see you."

I nodded.

"Why does your husband not want you to tell anyone?"

"I don't know. Since that time in his office, when you were there with those black men, he's changed. He's very curt with me."

"So I cannot discuss this with him," I said.

"No," she said. "I promised him."

"Promised him not to let him know you told anyone?"

"What's the difference," Beth said. "Will you help me?"

"Why not just leave him," I said. "Get out of town."

"And do what?" Beth said. "I'm thirty-four years old, and my only skill is undressing and lying on my back. Besides, that wouldn't protect him."

"Does he give you much money?" I said.

"He monitors every dime."

"So what about my fee?"

"Fee?"

"Yeah, I do this for a living," I said.

"I . . . But my life, our life, is in danger," Beth said.

"Can't you help her?" Estelle said. "Maybe we can find a way to pay you."

"Tell me more about the danger," I said.

"I don't know more," she said. "I know Chet does a lot of business with people he's never introduced me to. I know many of them are dangerous. And I know Chet is very . . . his word is *cute* . . . in his business practices."

"Boo and Zel still around?"

"They're taking care of Chet."

"Why not stay with Chet?"

"I can't stand to be with him like that all the time."

"And he's provided you no security?" I said.

"No. He doesn't seem to love me anymore."

"Hard to imagine," I said. "So you stay with him for the money. Why's he stay with you?"

"Sex."

"Well, as long as there's a bond," I said. "What would you want me to do?"

"Can't you provide security?"

"For no fee?" I said. "Twenty-four hours a day, seven days a week? For how long?"

"I . . . I don't know," she said.

I sat. The two women sat. I didn't like the story. Didn't mean it wasn't true. But I didn't like it.

"I need to think about this," I said.

"And what do I do while you're thinking?" Beth said.

"We'll go to a hotel," I said. "I'll register, and you'll stay there. I'll see that you're safe in the room. Room service, whatever. Estelle can stay with you if she wants to. When I go, you lock the door. And you don't open it for anybody until I come by for you in the morning . . . and we'll go from there."

"Will you stay with me?" Beth said.

"No."

"We could have an awfully good time if you did," Beth said.

"No," I said. "We couldn't."

Beth stood up suddenly.

"Oh, go to hell," she said.

She turned and stalked out of my office.

Estelle looked at me and shrugged and went after Beth.

I continued to sit at my desk. It was not clear to me what had just happened. On the other hand, it often wasn't, and I'd gotten used to it.

Chapter

44

I WAS IN FRANK BELSON'S CUBICLE at Boston police headquarters at Tremont and Ruggles.

"Found your name in a guy's Rolodex," Frank said.

"A dead guy?" I said.

"Wow," Belson said. "You figured that out because I'm a homicide cop?"

"Want to tell me who it is?" I said.

"Guy named Chester Jackson," Belson said.

I leaned back a little.

"I know him," I said.

"Tell me about him," Belson said.

"I gather he didn't die of natural causes," I said.

"Somebody put a forty-caliber slug into his head from about eight feet away, and a second one, from about three inches."

"To make sure," I said.

"Uh-huh."

"When did he get it?" I said.

"Secretary says he left his office at five p.m. Nine-one-one got an anonymous call at five-ten. Saying someone had been shot in the garage. There was a car in the area. It arrived at five-thirty, and there he was."

"What garage?" I said.

"Under International Place," Belson said. "'Bout two light years down."

"Was he parked there?"

"Yep. He was facedown on the floor with his car door open."

"So somebody was waiting for him," I said.

"This sounds more like me telling you than you telling me," Belson said.

"We'll get to me," I said.

Belson nodded.

"Yeah," he said. "We will."

"There's security in that garage, isn't there?"

"Yep. If you work there, you got a pass. If not, you have to be on a list."

"You got the list," I said.

"Amazingly, we thought of that," Belson said.

"Anything?"

"Not yet," Belson said. "Thought you might take a look."

"I will," I said. "If you walk into the lobby from the street and take the elevator down to the garage . . ."

"And aren't carrying something that looks like an infernal device," Belson said. "You're in."

"You'd be an idiot," I said, "to drive into the garage."

"Car was parked almost next to an elevator," Belson said.

"Assigned parking?"

"Yep. Sign says 'Reserved for C. Jackson.'"

"So," I said. "If you knew Jackson, you'd know he was a big deal and would be likely to have an assigned spot."

"So you could wander around the garage until you found it," Belson said.

"Probably be near an elevator, so maybe

you could cut down on the wandering," I said.

"And you wait there until he shows up," Belson said.

"Maybe," I said.

"Or you know him, you know where he parks, you know when he's going to come for his car, and you get there a few minutes early," Belson said. "And pop him."

"No witnesses," I said.

"Nope."

"No suspicious-looking people hanging around," I said.

"None reported."

"How come nobody ever sees a shooting?" I said.

"Shooter might try to arrange it that way," Belson said. "And it's a godsend for us. Give us something to do so that we're not in the bars drinking Jameson with a beer chaser by two in the afternoon."

"God is kind," I said.

"Tell me about Jackson," Belson said.

He had a notebook on the desk in front of him, and as I talked, every once in a while he wrote things in it.

"I don't know quite what he does, but I

know he makes a lot of dough, and I know all of it isn't clean."

"He wired?" Belson said.

"I would say so."

"Got any names?" Belson said.

"I know a name, but it's a guy just did me a favor, and unless I think he did Jackson, which I don't, I won't name him."

"We could insist," Belson said.

"You could," I said.

"We can be insistent as a sonovabitch," Belson said.

"I know."

"But you won't tell us anyway," Belson said.

"No."

"Known you a long time," Belson said.

"And yet here we are," I said. "Still in the bloom of youth."

Belson nodded.

"You get a suspicion," he said, "you let me know."

"At once," I said.

"Sure," Belson said. "I'll check with the organized-crime guys."

"I would," I said.

"What's your connection to him?"

I told him everything, as it was, except that I didn't name the other women. And I didn't mention Tony Marcus.

"And how did you resolve the problem?"

"Tireless negotiation," I said.

"Wife buy into it?" Belson said.

"She said she did."

"Think she might have not meant it."

"Probably," I said.

"Think she might have aced him?"

"She might have," I said. "But at the time Jackson was killed she was talking to me in my office with a woman named Estelle."

"What a coincidence," Belson said.

"It is," I said.

"Estelle who?"

"Don't know her last name. She's a trainer at Pinnacle Fitness."

"Want to tell me why they were there?"

"Beth said her life had been threatened and wanted me to protect her. Said her husband had been threatened, too. Estelle was there for moral support, I guess."

Belson wrote in the notebook.

"Were you planning on mentioning this?" he said.

"Sure," I said. "But I thought it would be

good training for you to learn of it through sound investigative procedure."

"Geez," Belson said. "With your help maybe I'll make lieutenant."

"I think you have to take the lieutenant's exam first," I said.

"I'll get to it," Belson said. "You want to tell me about the wife, what's her name"— he glanced at his notes—"Beth."

I told him about her visit the previous evening.

"You remember what the note said?"

"'Your husband had betrayed me,'" I said. "'For this you both shall die.'"

Belson wrote it down.

"Didn't seem to work out that way," he said.

"Shit happens," I said.

Belson nodded.

"You believe all of this?"

"I don't think so," I said.

"Think she might have been setting up an alibi?"

"Maybe," I said. "But if she was, was Estelle in it, too?"

"And Gary Cockhound?" Belson said.

"It was a fairly elaborate fake, if it was a fake," I said.

"The kind amateurs use," Belson said.

"True," I said.

"On the other hand, since she didn't actually do it," Belson said, "who did? Eisenhower?"

"I don't think so," I said.

"What's your gut tell you?" Belson said.

"My gut says there's something wrong with this," I said. "It also says that Gary Eisenhower isn't part of it."

Belson wrote in his notebook.

"On the other hand," he said, "your gut isn't too bright."

"True," I said. "Mostly it just knows when I'm hungry."

Chapter

✦✦

45

I SAT WITH BETH in her expensive off-white living room, which looked like it had been decorated by the pound. Beth was in a black dress that proclaimed her mourning and showed off her body.

"I'm sorry for your loss," I said.

"You told the police about me," she said.

"I did."

"That was mean," she said.

"No, it wasn't," I said. "I'm your alibi. You would have told them you were with me, and I would have confirmed it, and the cops would have said, 'How come you didn't tell us about her?'"

"Why do I need an alibi?" she said.

"You're the spouse of a murder victim."

"And that automatically makes me a suspect?" she said.

"They have to eliminate you," I said.

"I suppose," she said.

"Any thoughts on who might have done it?"

"I should think the warning note I showed you would be a clue," she said.

"Not much hard information," I said. "Do you still have the envelope?"

"Envelope?"

"That it came in."

"Oh, no," Beth said. "I threw it away. There was no return address or anything."

"Was it addressed in hand or typed or one of those little computer address stickers?"

"Hand," she said.

"Remember where it was postmarked?"

"Boston, maybe," she said. "I don't know. I'm not used to threatening letters. I'm not a detective. I just threw the envelope away."

"Sure," I said. "Nice outfit you're wearing."

"Oh, this, well, it's . . . I'm kind of in mourning. You think it's okay?"

"Swell," I said. "Are you his only heir?"

"There's a couple of ex-wives," she said. "No children. I'm the only one in the will."

"Well," I said. "There's a plus."

"It is a plus," she said. "But there's no need for you to be so snarky about it. My husband has just been murdered."

"True," I said.

"I mean, we had our problems, sure. . . ."

"And now you don't," I said.

She was sitting on the ivory-colored couch. I was sitting on a straight-backed armchair across from her. She squared her shoulders and sat more upright.

"Do you suspect me?" she said.

"I remain open-minded," I said.

"What a terrible thing to say. It's disgusting that you could even think that."

"Disgusting," I said.

"Why do you even care?" she said. "Has someone hired you to work on this case?"

"No," I said.

"Then why don't you go off somewhere and be disgusting on someone else's business."

"I've been involved with this for a while,"

I said. "It's my line of work. I feel some obligation to see what I can do."

"Well, don't think you have any obligation to me," Beth said. "I'd like it if I never saw you again."

"You, too?" I said.

Chapter

·❖·

46

I SPENT THE WEEKEND at Susan's place, where, after some early morning excitement, we usually sat in her kitchen and had a lingering Sunday brunch prepared mostly by me. This morning was a little different; we were having scrambled eggs prepared by Susan. It was one of her two specialties, the other being boiled water. I added a ragout of peppers, onions, and mushrooms to grace the plate, and we ate it with oatmeal toast. Pearl came from her spot on the living-room couch and joined us, alert for any spillage.

"I talked with Beth Jackson on Friday," I said.

"Are you still suspicious of her?"

"Let me recount our discussion," I said.

"I'm all ears," Susan said.

"Actually," I said. "Not all."

She smiled, and I gave her, almost verbatim, my conversation with Beth.

"You like to show off that you can do that," Susan said. "Don't you."

"Yes," I said. "Is there anything bothersome about what you heard."

"Your voice was sexually exciting?" Susan said.

"Besides that," I said.

"In relation to the murder," Susan said.

"Yes."

Susan was silent, her mind running over the conversation.

"Remember why she came to me the night of the murder," I said.

"She wanted you to protect her," Susan said. "And, at least peripherally, her husband."

"Correct," I said.

"And now"—Susan began to speak faster, trying to keep up with her mind— "when half the threat has been executed, she should be more desperate for protection."

"Bingo," I said.

"And she isn't," Susan said. "She doesn't want to ever see you again."

"Or words to that effect," I said.

"Which would lead a trained observer," Susan said, "to conclude that she no longer thought there was a threat."

"It might," I said. "Or she might have found me so disgusting that she preferred to look elsewhere for protection."

"No," Susan said. "Not if she's in fear of her life. However disgusting she may have found you, you are also safety. She would have embraced you."

"Who wouldn't," I said.

"I was speaking metaphorically," Susan said.

"Oh," I said.

"But we know she didn't do it herself," Susan said.

"I can vouch for that," I said. "In fact, it seems too carefully done. She comes to me at five. At five-ten an anonymous caller reports a shooting, cops are there by five-thirty. Beth doesn't leave my office until about six."

"A lot of people could have made an anonymous call," Susan said. "They saw it happen but didn't want to be involved."

"Nine-one-one records all call numbers. This one was from a disposable phone."

"They can't trace it?"

"Correct," I said.

"So it could have been someone who just happened to use a disposable phone, or it could have been a deliberate way to avoid identification."

"How many people you know that carry disposable phones?" I said.

"Nobody."

"Guy also tried to disguise his voice. Belson said it's a man speaking in a falsetto."

"So it could have been the murderer," Susan said.

"Could have been," I said.

"But why would he call the police? Wouldn't it be in his better interest not to?"

"One would think," I said.

"Unless he wanted to establish that the murder took place while Beth was with you," Susan said.

"Which means she was involved," I said.

"Or Estelle," Susan said.

"Or both," I said.

"Why would Estelle be involved?"

"Why do people usually kill other people?" I said.

"Mostly over love or money," Susan said.

"If Estelle's involved," I said, "it wouldn't be about love."

"You can't be sure," Susan said. "Human emotion is sometimes very convolute."

"I've heard that," I said.

Susan smiled and drank some coffee.

"How about Gary Eisenhower?" she said.

"You think he might do that?" I said.

"No," Susan said.

"Shrink insight or woman's intuition?" I said.

"Sometimes there's not much difference," Susan said.

"I don't think he did it, either," I said.

"Gumshoe insight?" Susan said. "Or male intuition?"

I grinned at her.

"Sometimes," I said, "there's not much difference."

"Does he have an alibi?" Susan said.

"Don't know," I said. "Belson was supposed to interview him today."

"So," Susan said, "pending what you get

from Belson, if it wasn't Gary, who did the actual shooting?"

"Damn," I said. "You don't know that, either?"

"Sorry," Susan said.

"And you a Harvard Ph.D."

"I know," Susan said. "Puzzling, isn't it."

Chapter

47

GARY EISENHOWER CAME to my office on Monday morning, while I was reading the paper.

"You know," I said, as he sat down. "I don't think I've ever disagreed with anything in Doonesbury."

"Doonesbury?"

"Guy's always on the money," I said.

"Yeah, right," Gary said. "Beth Jackson's husband got killed."

"I know that," I said.

"You know anything more?" Gary said.

"He was shot twice in the head in the

parking garage at International Place," I said.

"They know who did it?"

"No."

"They got any suspects?" Gary said.

"No."

"What about Beth?"

"She's got an ironclad alibi," I said.

"No, I mean, is she safe?"

"Don't know," I said.

"You're not giving her security?"

"Nope."

"But," Gary said, "the letter said both of them, and obviously they meant it."

"She told me to get lost," I said.

"Don't you hate when that happens," Gary said.

"You get used to it," I said.

Gary grinned.

"Wouldn't know," he said. "I see Boo around, maybe he's looking out for her."

"Boo?"

"Yeah."

"Without Zel?" I said.

"Haven't seen Zel," Gary said. "Maybe they broke up."

I nodded.

"Cops talk to you yet?" I said.

"Yeah," he said. "Detective named Belson."

"How'd that go," I said.

"I'm clear," he said. "I was cultivating a new client. Belson talked with her. Told her he saw no need to involve her husband."

"New client a member at Pinnacle Fitness?"

He smiled.

"Sure," he said. "Thing keeps working, you don't go to something else."

"You seen Beth," I said. "Since the murder?"

"Yeah. She's not devastated."

"She got the money," I said.

"Yep, and she's talking about her and me picking up again."

"So you're not exactly devastated," I said.

"Money's good," he said. "But I kind of like it when they ain't free as a bird, you know? They got a husband and don't want to leave him, makes everything work better for me."

"How's Estelle feel about Beth?" I said.

"She likes her," Gary said.

"She doesn't mind your client list?" I said.

"Naw," Gary said. "Estelle's pretty cool. The whole blackmail scheme was more hers than mine, tell you the truth."

"Really?"

"Yeah," Gary said. "She used to do some videotape work, training clients, you know?"

"So the hidden cameras were her doing," I said.

"Yeah," Gary said. "Behind every successful man . . ."

"And she doesn't mind sharing you with other women," I said.

"No," Gary said. "She . . ." He paused. "The first time we started using the hidden cameras and the voice recorders, it was for her."

"You mean so she could watch and listen?"

"Yeah," Gary said. "It turns her on."

I nodded.

"How'd you feel about it?" I said.

"Well, you know, it was a little creepy at first."

He looked at the back of his hands for a moment. Then he looked up and smiled.

"But I'm a laid-back guy."

"And your partners in bed?" I said.

"What they don't know won't hurt them was the way we looked at it."

"Until you started the blackmail."

"It was a good parlay for us," Gary said.

"You and Estelle."

"Yeah," Gary said. "In most deals there's winners and losers, you know?"

"And your clients were the losers."

"I suppose," Gary said. "But nobody got hurt very bad. They liked the sex. I liked the sex. They were married to money. I only wanted some of it. Estelle and me were living pretty high up on the hog. Hell, Beth still wants to be with me, and, by the way, so does Abigail Larson."

I nodded.

"Abigail's a drinker," Gary said.

"Yep."

"Estelle says it makes her unreliable, and we shouldn't waste time with her."

"She still giving you money?"

"Naw, I . . ." He paused. "I'm a little embarrassed, but I sort of gave you my word on the blackmail."

"So you won't take her money?"

"Nope. Beth's, either. I mean, before her husband got killed."

"But you're still having sex," I said.

"Yeah," he said. "I figured that wasn't part of the promise."

"I like a man with standards," I said.

Chapter

❖

48

I FOUND ZEL AND BOO sharing a two-bedroom apartment in Jamaica Plain. There was linoleum on all the floors and a soapstone sink in the kitchen. Zel answered the door.

"Come in," Zel said. And nodded toward one of the empty chairs at the kitchen table. "Have a seat."

Boo was seated at the kitchen table, in his undershirt, reading *The Herald*. He stood when Zel let me in and left the room. Zel watched him go and put his hand out to stop me and stood between me and the door that Boo had left through. In a moment Boo returned with a gun.

"Put it away, Boo," Zel said.

Boo pointed the gun at us.

"Get out of the way," he said to Zel.

"Put it away," Zel said, and walked slowly toward Boo, keeping himself between us.

I focused on the gun in Boo's hand. It was a semiautomatic, maybe a .40-caliber. The hammer was back. His finger was on the trigger. If I saw any sign of finger movement I would go down and roll. I adjusted slightly to keep Zel between us.

"Get out of the way, Zel," Boo said again.

Zel took another step and reached out and took hold of the gun. Boo stared at him, his face squeezed tight, then let Zel take it. Zel eased the hammer down and put the gun in his hip pocket.

"I do the gun work, Boo," Zel said. "You know that."

Boo nodded slowly, then turned and left the room again.

"He got another gun?" I said.

"No," Zel said. "He's going in there to sulk."

"How bad is he?" I said.

"In the head?" Zel said, and shrugged. "You saw him, he drops his hands when he fights. He always has."

"So he's had his brain rattled."

"A lot," Zel said.

"Can he take care of himself?"

"Not against a guy like you," Zel said. "Amateurs, he does fine. He can still punch."

"I meant can he take care of himself in general," I said. "You know, buy food, balance his checkbook, go to the dentist?"

"I take care of him," Zel said.

"Been doing that long?"

"Yeah."

We sat for a minute. Zel sat across the table from me, where he could watch the door to the room that Boo had gone to.

"You got any work now that Jackson got aced?" I said.

"Not right now, but I'm making some calls. People know me."

"Seen Mrs. Jackson at all?"

"Not since her old man got whacked," Zel said.

"Know why Jackson got whacked?" I said.

"No."

"Know who did it?"

"No."

"Any suggestions?" I said.

"How'd he get it," Zel said. "I know he got shot, but cops wouldn't tell me anything else."

"Two in the head," I said. "One from about eight feet. One from about three inches."

"Proves it ain't me. The one from eight feet woulda been enough."

"That a forty-caliber you took away from Boo?" I said.

"Never noticed," Zel said. "Jackson capped with a forty."

"Yep."

"Boo ain't much of a shooter," Zel said.

"From eight feet you don't have to be much of a shooter," I said.

"You any good?" Zel said.

"Yes," I said.

"Know anybody better?"

"Two guys," I said. "Vinnie Morris, guy from L.A. named Chollo . . . maybe Hawk."

"That's three," Zel said.

"So maybe three," I said.

"I hearda Vinnie Morris," Zel said.

"You as good as Vinnie," I said.

"Ain't been determined," Zel said.

"How come you weren't with Jackson

when he got shot," I said. "I sorta thought that was your job."

"Told us to take the day off," Zel said. "Said he didn't need us."

"Was Boo with you when Jackson was shot?" I said.

"Boo's always with me," Zel said.

"I'd swear that gun you took from Boo was a forty," I said.

Zel took it out and looked at it.

"Nice call," he said. "S-and-W forty-caliber."

"Yours?" I said.

"They're all mine," Zel said. "I don't want Boo carrying no gun."

"How many you got?" I said.

"Six," Zel said.

"All of them clean as this one?" I said.

"I keep them clean," Zel said.

"Tools of the trade," I said.

"Sure," he said.

I looked at the door to the room where Boo was sulking.

"Too bad Boo never learned to keep his hands up," I said.

"Everybody tried," Zel said. "But when the fight started, he could never remember.

Even before he got hit, Boo wasn't the brightest guy you'd meet."

I nodded. We sat again.

"I hear anything useful," Zel said, "I'll give you a shout."

"Please do," I said.

Chapter

49

I SAT WITH ESTELLE at the café counter in Pinnacle Fitness. I had coffee, and Estelle drank green tea. I didn't care. I was still bigger and stronger than she was. The hell with green tea.

"Are you working on the murder case?" she said.

"I am."

Estelle was wearing the tight black sweats and the tight white tank top that was apparently the Pinnacle trainer's uniform.

"Who hired you?"

"I'm working on spec," I said.

She looked at me as if I might be odd.

"Do the police have a suspect?" she said.

"No."

"Have they had any success tracking the note?" she said. "You know, fingerprints? What machine it was written on? Kind of paper?"

"You've been watching those crime-scene shows," I said. "Haven't you."

She smiled.

"Especially the one with David Caruso." She glanced at me sideways. "He's hot."

"Hotter than myself?" I said.

"Oh, yes," she said. "Of course."

She must have had a thing for slim, handsome guys. How shallow.

"It was written on a computer," I said. "Printed out on paper you can buy at any Staples. No fingerprints that mean anything."

" 'Mean anything'?"

"Well, yours are on it, and Gary's and Beth's, and mine," I said. "That's because we handled it. There are no unaccounted-for prints."

"Oh."

She thought about it for a while.

Then she said, "So how do you solve a crime like this?"

"You don't always," I said.

"But, I mean, how would you even go about it?" she said. "There's, like, no clues."

"You talk to people," I said. "You ask them questions. You listen to their answers. You compare what they said to what other people have said. You try to assess body language. You try to listen for tone."

"Is that what you're doing now?" Estelle said.

"Yes."

"How am I doing?" she said.

"You're not telling me anything, but it is sort of enjoyable to study your body language."

"Enjoyable?"

"It's a dandy body," I said.

"Oh," she said. "Thank you."

"You don't really think I did it?" she said.

"I don't think," I said. "I just ask questions and listen to answers and study bodies."

"I'll bet you think," Estelle said.

"Mostly about sex and baseball," I said. "How's Beth?"

"I am not interested in baseball," she said, and looked at me sideways again.

"Good to know," I said. "How's Beth?"

Estelle's face became serious.

"Poor thing," Estelle said. "She's devastated."

I nodded.

"Devastated," I said.

"Yes, to have your husband murdered?" Estelle said. "You don't think that's devastating?"

"Never had a husband," I said.

"She's staying with us for a while," Estelle said.

"'Us'?"

"Me and Gary," Estelle said.

"You and Gary and Beth," I said.

"You have a problem with that?"

I shook my head.

"Not my problem," I said.

She frowned, though it seemed to me that she was careful that it be a pretty frown.

"It's nobody's problem," she said. "Unless you're some kind of mossback puritan."

"Goddamn," I said. "You've seen through my disguise."

Chapter

❖❖

50

Beth and Gary and Estelle?" Susan said.

We were having coffee in her kitchen on a Monday morning, before she went to work.

"So it seems," I said.

Susan was in her understated tailored suit, working attire that did its best to conceal the fact that she was gorgeous. Her makeup was quiet; her hair was neat. She wore very little jewelry. And she remained gorgeous.

"If I weren't a sophisticated psychotherapist with advanced degrees from

Harvard, I might be faintly shocked," she said.

"They didn't do three-ways in Swampscott?" I said.

"When I was in high school," Susan said, "I doubt that anyone in town knew what a three-way was."

"We're not in high school anymore, Toto," I said.

"Did they know in Laramie?" Susan said. "When you were a kid?"

"Of course," I said.

"Truly?" Susan said.

"Two heifers and a seed bull," I said.

"I sometimes forget you're a man of the West," Susan said.

"Howdy."

Susan smiled. She was eating half of a whole-wheat bagel. I settled for several cinnamon donuts.

"Could you perform in a three-way?" Susan said.

"Two women and me?"

"For instance," Susan said.

"Maybe," I said. "You?"

"No," Susan said. "How about two men and a woman?"

"No," I said.

"Me, either," Susan said.

"So," I said. "Lucky we found each other."

She smiled.

"It has been my experience that at least one member of a threesome is uncomfortable with the deal," Susan said.

"So why do it?" I said.

"To please one, or both, of the other partners," Susan said. "To convince oneself of one's liberation and openness, fear of being a prude."

"Vive la prudery," I said.

Susan nodded.

"You think it can sometimes work?" I said.

"Yes," Susan said. "I think people can often successfully be in a functioning relationship with two other people. You know, that sort of traditional European thing. Husband, wife, and husband's mistress . . . or wife's lover . . . or all of the above."

"Ménage à trois?" I said.

Susan shrugged.

"That seems to be Gary and the girls," I said.

Susan nodded.

"What do you think?" I said.

"I would have more hope for it if there was some separation," she said.

"Gary lives with one and visits the other?" I said.

"Or all three live separately," Susan said. "Despite what people say, and even believe, if they are genuinely invested in someone, it is more difficult to share that person with another than they expect."

"So it works better if you don't have to have your nose rubbed in it, so to speak," I said.

"Yes."

"Do you think it's healthy?" I said.

"Healthy is harder to pin down than it seems," Susan said.

She had slid into her professional mode—probably the suit.

"I know a number of people who maintain a happy and productive life with two partners, not under the same roof."

"Think it'll work for Gary and friends?" I said.

"There's something exploitive going on there, I think," Susan said.

"I think so, too," I said. "So?"

"No," Susan said.

"Think we should try it?"

"Who would the other guy be?" Susan said.

"Woman," I said.

"We can't even decide who'd have the extra lover," Susan said.

I nodded.

"How about neither?" I said.

Susan sipped her coffee, and put down her cup, and carefully blotted her lips with her napkin. The she looked at me and smiled widely. I put my right hand up, and she high-fived me.

"There you go," she said.

Chapter

51

BELSON AND I sat in Belson's car outside a Dunkin' Donuts on Gallivan Boulevard, drinking coffee and browsing a box of assorted donuts. I preferred the plain ones. Belson liked the ones with strawberry frosting and sprinkles.

"What kind of sissy eats strawberry-frosted donuts?" I said.

"With jimmies," Belson said.

"I had too much respect for you," I said, "even to mention the jimmies."

"Thanks," Belson said. "My poetic side."

"Um," I said.

"You know that Jackson's widow has moved in with your boy Goran?"

"And his girlfriend," I said.

"What the fuck is that about?" Belson said.

"Love?" I said.

Belson looked at me as if I had just spit up.

"They did the will," Belson said. "She is now worth eighty million, seven hundred, and twenty-three bucks."

"More or less," I said.

"That's the number they gave me," Belson said. "I assume it's rounded to the nearest dollar."

"Might explain why Estelle and Gary have welcomed her into their home," I said.

"But why does she want to go?" Belson said.

"Why do most people do anything?" I said.

"Love or money, or variations on either," Belson said.

"She don't seem to need money," I said.

"So we're back to love," Belson said.

"But you don't like it," I said.

"I don't see that broad doing anything for love," Belson said.

"You don't like Beth?" I said.

"I think she killed her husband," Belson said.

"Not herself," I said.

"No, but there's people who'll do any-thing you need if you have money."

"She didn't have it until her husband died," I said.

"So maybe she got a trusting hit guy," Belson said.

"Like who?" I said.

Belson shrugged.

"Don't know any trusting hit guys," he said.

We were quiet. Belson ate the last strawberry-frosted.

"Love and money," he said.

"Or sex and money," I said.

"Same thing," Belson said.

"You think they took it out in trade?" I said.

"It's what she's got," Belson said.

"And it's gotten her this far," I said.

"So it's a theory," Belson said.

He found a chocolate-cream donut un-der a cinnamon one, and took it out from under and dusted off the accidental cin-namon and took a careful bite. The donut had a squishy filling, and Belson was very neat.

"She know anybody would kill somebody?" Belson said.

"Her husband did," I said. "She probably met some. She knew Boo and Zel."

"I'll keep it in mind," Belson said.

"Doesn't explain why she's living with Gary and Estelle," I said.

"Nope," Belson said.

I located the cinnamon donut that Belson had put aside in favor of chocolate cream. We ate silently for a moment.

"We don't have any idea what we're doing," I said.

"No," Belson said. "We don't seem to."

Chapter

❖❖

52

I OPENED THE BPD FOLDER on Beth. She had been born Elizabeth Boudreau in a shabby little town on the Merrimack River, east of Proctor. She was thirty-six. In the month she graduated from Tarbridge High School, she married a guy name Boley LaBonte, and divorced him a year later.

Nobody was paying me to do anything. On the other hand, no one was paying me to do nothing, either. Business was slow. I was nosy. And I had kind of a bad feeling about this long-running mess I'd wandered into and hadn't done a hell of a lot to improve. So I got my car from the alley where I had a deal with the meter maids, and headed north from Boston on a very nice February day with the temperature above freezing and stuff melting gently.

You enter Tarbridge on a two-lane highway from the south. The town is basically three unpainted cinder-block buildings and a red light. A few clapboard houses, some with paint, dwindle away from the cinder block. Up a hill past the red light, maybe a half-mile away, stood a regal-looking red-brick high school. The fact that Tarbridge had a municipal identity was stretching it a bit. That it had a high school was jaw-dropping. It had to be a regional school. But why they had located a regional high school in Tarbridge could only have to do with available land, or, of course, graft.

The town clerk was a fat woman with a red face and a tight perm. She had her offices in a trailer attached to one of the cinder-block buildings. The plastic nameplate on her desk said she was Mrs. Estevia Root.

I handed her my card, and she studied it through some pink-rimmed glasses with rhinestones on them, which hung around her neck on what appeared to be a cut-down shoelace.

"What do ya wanna see Mrs. Boudreau for?" the clerk said.

"I'm investigating a case," I said. "In Boston."

"Boston?"

"Uh-huh."

"What the hell are you doing up here?"

"Just background stuff," I said. "Where would I find Mrs. Boudreau."

"Probably in her kitchen, where she usually is."

"And where is the kitchen located?"

"Back of the house," Estevia said.

I nodded happily.

"And the house?" I said.

"Passed it on the way in, if you come from Boston," Estevia said. "'Bout a hundred yards back, be on your right heading out. Kinda run-down, looks empty, but she'll be in there."

I felt a chill. If Estevia thought it looked run-down . . .

"Did you happen to know her daughter?" I said. "Beth?"

"She run off long time ago, and no loss," Estevia said.

"No loss?"

"Best she was gone, 'fore she dragged half the kids in town down with her."

"Bad girl?" I said.

Estevia's mouth became a thin, hard line. Her round face seemed to plane into angles.

"Yes," she said.

"Bad how?" I said.

"Just bad," Estevia said.

It was all I was going to get from Estevia.

"Thank you for your time," I said.

Chapter

❖❖

53

IT WAS A very small house. It not only looked empty, it looked like it should be empty. There wasn't enough paint left on the front to indicate what color it might once have been. The roofline was bowed. The windows were closed and dirty. Something that might once have been curtains hung in tattered disarray in the windows.

I parked and went to the front door. There was no path shoveled. The uncut weeds of summer, now long dead, stuck up through the diminishing snow. There was no doorknob, and the hole where there had been one was plugged with a rag. I knocked. No one answered. I pushed on the door. It didn't move. I'm not sure it was locked; it was more likely just warped shut.

I went around to the side of the house and found what might be a kitchen door. There was a screen door and an inner door. The screening had torn loose and was curled up along one side. The inner door had a glass window that was so grimy, I couldn't see through it. I knocked.

From inside somebody croaked, "Go 'way."

It didn't sound welcoming, but I figured the somebody didn't really mean it, so I opened the inside door and stepped in. She looked like a huge sack of soiled laundry, slouched inertly at the kitchen table, drinking Pastene port wine from a small jelly glass with cartoon pictures on it. The table was covered with linoleum whose color and design were long since lost. There were pots and dishes in the soapstone sink, piles of newspapers and magazines in various corners. A small television with rabbit ears was playing jaggedly. The scripted conviviality and canned laughter was eerie in the desperate room. A black iron stove stood against the far wall, and the room reeked of kerosene and heat.

"Mrs. Boudreau?" I said.

"Go 'way," she croaked again.

She was very fat, wearing some sort of robe or housedress. It was hard to tell, and in truth, I didn't look very closely.

"My name is Spenser," I said, and handed her a card. She didn't take it, so I put it on the table.

"You're Elizabeth Boudreau's mother," I said.

Her glass was empty. She picked up the bottle of port with both hands and carefully poured it into the jelly glass. She put the bottle down carefully, and picked up the glass carefully with both hands and sipped the port. Then she looked at me as if I hadn't spoken.

"Could you tell me a little about Elizabeth?" I said.

"Elizabeth."

"Your daughter."

"Gone," the woman said.

"Elizabeth's gone?"

Mrs. Boudreau nodded.

"Long time," she said.

"What can you tell me about her?" I said.

"Bitch," her mother said.

I nodded. If Beth was thirty-six, this woman was probably sixty, maybe younger. She looked older than Angkor Wat.

"Why bitch?" I said.

"Whore."

This wasn't going terribly well.

"How about Mr. Boudreau?" I said.

She drank port and stared at me.

"He around?" I said.

"No."

"Dead?"

"Don't know."

"Can you tell me anything about him?" I said.

"Bastard," she said.

"Could you tell me where to find him?"

"No."

I had hung around in this reeking trash bin as long as I could stand it. There was nothing I could find out that would be worth staying any longer.

"Thank you," I said, and turned and went out.

I took in some big breaths as I walked to my car. The air felt clean.

Chapter

54

BOLEY LABONTE OWNED a bowling alley and lounge called Kingpin Lanes, which sat in the middle of a big parking lot on South Tarbridge Road. There were two pickups and an old Buick sedan parked outside. Inside, four guys were bowling together. In the lounge three other guys were sitting at the bar, drinking beer and watching a woman with few clothes on dancing at a brass pole to music I neither recognized nor liked. It was two o'clock in the afternoon.

I sat at the bar and ordered a beer. The bartender was a red-haired woman with an angular face and skin you could strike a match on.

"Boley around?" I said.

"Who wants to know?" the bartender said.

I gave her my card, the understated one, where my name was not spelled out in bullet holes. She looked at it.

"A freaking private eye?" she said.

"Exactly," I said.

"Why you want to talk with Boley?"

"None of your business," I said.

"Yeah, I guess not," she said, and took the card and walked down to the end of the bar and ducked under, which was not easy given how tight her jeans were. She opened a door marked *Office* and went in; a moment later she came out and ducked back behind the bar.

"Boley says he'll be right out," she said.

I nodded and sipped my beer. The girl on the pole was a kid, maybe eighteen, nineteen, looking deadly serious, starting her long climb to stardom. A man came out of the office and walked down the bar and sat on the stool next to me.

"How ya doin'," he said. "I'm Boley La-Bonte."

We shook hands.

"I'm looking into a case involving Elizabeth Boudreau," I said. "I understand you were married to her."

He had dark, curly hair, worn sort of long and brushed back. He had a thin mustache. His flowered shirt was unbuttoned to his sternum, showing a hairy chest and a gold chain. The material of the shirt stretched a little tight over his biceps.

"That was a trip," he said.

"What can you tell me about her?" I said.

"Jesus," he said, and looked at the bartender. "Mavis, gimme a Coke."

She put it in front of him, and he drank some and looked at my beer bottle.

"You okay?" he said.

I said I was.

"Beth Boudreau," he said. "I heard she's doing good."

"Married money," I said.

"Good for her," Boley said. "You know anything about where she come from?"

"I talked with her mother this morning," I said.

"Alberta?" Boley said. "She still alive?"

"Sort of," I said. "Is there a Mr. Boudreau?"

"Nope," Boley said. "Never was. Alberta got knocked up."

"Jesus," I said.

"Yeah," Boley said. "Hard to think about." I nodded.

"Anyway," Boley said. "Alberta Boudreau was always fat and homely, and my old man says never had a date. Then one day she comes up pregnant. It was a joke in town, Alberta was one for one, you know?"

"Who was the father?"

"Don't know. Nobody seems to," he said. He drank some more Coke.

"This ain't Boston," he said. "Or Cambridge. Everybody's like shocked back, what? Thirty-six years ago, something like that. But goddamn, Alberta has the kid. Everybody thought she had it to prove she'd gotten laid."

"Could be other reasons," I said.

"Could be," Boley said.

He finished his Coke, and the bartender delivered a second one without being asked.

"How they get along?" I said.

"Beth and her mother?" Boley said. "Don't know. Don't know anybody was ever in the house."

"I was," I said.

Boley made a face.

"I don't want to know," he said.

"No," I said. "You don't. How about school. Beth catch any grief about all this in school?"

"I dunno. I'm ten years older than her. But . . ." He drank some Coke. "You know how school is."

"I do," I said. "How'd you meet her?"

"She was working the pole here," Boley said. "At the time, I'm the bouncer. Used to box a little—Golden Gloves and stuff." He shrugged. "Good enough for here."

"And now you own it," I said.

"Yeah," Boley said. "Guy owned it was a lush, he was going under. My old man died, left me a little insurance dough. I got it cheap."

"Great country," I said.

Boley was looking at me.

"You used to fight," he said. "Am I right?"

"Yep."

"It's the nose, mostly," Boley said. "And around the eyes. Ever fight pro?"

"Yep."

"Heavy?"

"Uh-huh."

"You good?" Boley said.

"I was good," I said. "Not great."

"So you was never gonna be champ," Boley said.

"No."

"But I bet you ain't lost many on the street," Boley said.

"Not many," I said.

"Thing about boxing," Boley said, "you know. You may not win, but you got a plan."

I nodded.

"And," Boley said, "when you box, you learn that getting hit ain't the end of the fucking world."

I nodded again.

"Just another day at the office," I said.

He grinned. We were quiet for a time, watching the girl making love to the brass pole.

"Beth was like that kid," Boley said. "She come here thinking she was a performer, you know? Thinking this was her ticket out of Palookaville."

"But it wasn't," I said.

"Not from dancing," he said.

"You sleep with her?" I said.

"Course," Boley said. The bartender brought him another Coke. "Sleep with them all, part of the deal. I hire 'em to strip for the customers and fuck the owner." He grinned. "Which is me."

"You sleeping with this kid?" I said.

"Sure."

"How old is she?"

"She's eighteen," Boley said. "Gotta be eighteen to do this, and I'm careful about that."

"Any of the dancers freelance with the clients?"

"On their own time," he said. "Not on mine. Don't look like much now, but most nights we're jumping. It's a nice business for me. I'm not gonna hire anybody underage. I'm not gonna serve anybody underage. I'm not gonna allow no soliciting on my premises."

I nodded.

"You still bouncing?" I said.

He shook his head.

"I hire it done now," he said.

"How was the marriage?"

He shrugged.

"She was hot enough," he said. "And she tried to be nice to me. I mean, I was not only her husband, I was her income, you know?"

"She still, ah, dance?"

"No, I wouldn't tolerate that when she was married to me."

"Propriety," I said.

"Whatever. But the thing I always knew was she didn't like me. It was . . . she liked to fuck me, but she resented the rest of it. And man, did she have a temper. Come a point it would blow and she couldn't control it."

"That why you divorced?" I said.

"Nope."

"Why'd you divorce?" I said.

"She was fucking other people," he said. "I cut her loose."

I nodded.

"You know where she went next?" I said.

"Nope."

"You get married again?"

"Yep. Nice woman. I didn't meet her here. Two daughters. Nice house in Andover," he said.

"Your wife understand the arrangement with the strippers?" I said.

Boley grinned at me.

"Don't ask," he said. "Don't tell."

The music stopped. The kid on the

pole stopped dancing and, wearing only a G-string, walked unself-consciously off the stage.

"At night the G-string goes," Boley said. "But I ain't wasting it in the middle of the afternoon on a couple shitkickers in down vests."

"It's a hard life," I said.

"It is, and most of them are too stupid to do anything else," he said.

"Hard for Beth," I said.

"Hard for everybody," Boley said. "You need to be tough if you're gonna get any-where."

"And smart," I said.

"Yeah," Boley said. "That helps."

"You think Beth was smart?" I said.

"She was tough, okay," he said. "But she didn't know much."

"You can be smart and not know much," I said.

He nodded and drank some Coke.

"Smartest broad I ever fucked," he said.

And that in itself must be some kind of fame.

Chapter

❖

55

THIS ONE GOT Quirk's interest. He stood with Belson and me, looking down at the body of Estelle, facedown near the edge of the Frog Pond in the Common.

"According to the contents of her purse," Belson said, "her name is Estelle Galla- gher. And she works at Pinnacle, where she is a certified physical trainer."

"Appears to be the same Estelle," I said.

She had been shot by someone who had apparently put the gun right up against the back of her head. She'd been shot twice. The second time probably as she lay facedown on the ground. One of the bullets had exited her face somewhere in the area of her nose, and it rendered a visual ID problematic. The three of us looked down at her in the harsh light of the crime-scene lamps. It made everything bright enough so that the crime-scene people could scoot about with cameras and tape measures and brushes and powders, and various kits containing nothing I understood. Several Boston cops, of lesser rank than Quirk, were going over the area foot by foot.

"Estelle Gallagher," I said. "Never knew her last name."

"Don't look Irish," Quirk said.

"No disgrace to it," I said.

"Not now," Quirk said.

He turned and walked to where a uniformed guy was standing with Gary and Beth. I followed him. Beth was holding on to Gary's arm with both of hers. She was crying.

"I'm sorry for your loss," Quirk said.

"It's terrible," Beth said.

Gary looked dazed.

"Do you have any thoughts on who or why?" Quirk said.

"No," Beth said, and cried some more.

"You, sir?" Quirk said to Gary.

He shook his head slowly.

"No one had any reason to do this to Estelle," he said.

His voice was flat and not very loud. He looked as if Beth's clutch on his arm was weighing him down.

"She lived with you two," Quirk said pleasantly.

"Yes," Beth said. "She was a friend."

"She was my girlfriend," Gary said in the same affectless voice. "Been my girlfriend a long time."

Quirk didn't say anything.

"When's the last time you saw her?" he said. "Either of you?"

They looked at each other as if to compare notes.

"This morning," Gary said. Beth nodded. "Before she went to the club. I was having some breakfast with her. Beth was still in, weren't you?"

"Yes," she said, still sniffling. "But I heard you talking. I actually last *saw* her last night before I went to bed."

Quirk nodded and looked at Belson.

"Frank," he said. "We got a time of death yet?"

"Nope."

"Okay, get a statement from these folks, and when the time of death is established, see if they got an alibi."

"Alibi?" Beth said. "You think one of us would do this?"

"Course not," Quirk said. "But it would be comforting to know you couldn't have."

He jerked his head at me and walked away.

When we were far enough away to talk, he said, "What's this fucking threesome?"

"You may have nailed it," I said.

"A fucking threesome?"

"Yeah."

"And they all knew about each other?"

"I think so," I said.

"I'm not sure any of the nuns at Saint Anthony's told me about this," he said.

"Probably not," I said.

"First her husband, now her, ah, roommate. I was this Eisenhower guy, I'd be a little careful walking around with old Beth."

"Or she with him," I said.

"Or she with him," Quirk said. "Tell me what you know."

Which I did.

Chapter

56

WE IN A MARRIOTT HOTEL," Hawk said. "In Burlington fucking Massachusetts."

We were in a new restaurant called Summer Winter.

"Susan says it's great," I said.

Susan smiled at him and nodded. Hawk looked around the room.

"Don't see no brothers," Hawk said.

"I know," Susan said.

They grinned at each other. Sometimes they communicated on levels even I didn't quite get. Hawk looked at me.

"What you know from the po-lice," he said.

"Gun killed Estelle was the same as the gun that killed Jackson," I said.

"Thing keeps getting more incestuous," Hawk said. "Don't it."

"It do," I said.

The waitress brought our drink order. She was pleasant to all of us. Though she was, perhaps, a little extra-pleasant to Hawk.

Hawk sipped from his margarita.

"Beth and Eisenhower got an alibi?" he said.

I nodded.

"They were together at some sort of fund-raiser cocktail party at The Langham Hotel," I said. "Twenty people saw them."

"Too bad," Hawk said.

"You think they're involved?" Susan said.

"Ah is just a poor simple bad guy," Hawk said, "trying to get along. Ask the dee-tective."

"Who else is there?" I said.

"Couldn't it be a party or parties un-known?" Susan said.

"Sure," I said. "But on the assumption of same gun, same shooter, they would need to be connected to both Estelle and Jackson."

"They have alibis for both," Susan said.

"Rock-solid," I said. "For both."

Susan guzzled nearly a full gram of her martini.

"Suppose," I said, "that someone you knew was murdered yesterday evening, and the cops asked you for an alibi."

"I washed my hair," Susan said. "Took a bath, put on some night cream, and got in bed with Pearl and watched a movie on HBO."

"And if they asked what movie, and could you remember the plot?"

"I could tell them that, but the movie has been running all month on my cable system," Susan said.

"So Pearl is basically your alibi," I said.

"Hawk?" I said.

"There be a young woman . . ." Hawk said.

"Of course there was," I said.

I drank some of my short scotch and soda.

"Last night I had a couple of cocktails," I said. "Made supper, ate it, and watched the first half of the Celtics game before I fell asleep."

"So you don't even have Pearl," Susan said.

"I don't," I said.

"So you're saying that people often don't have any way to prove where they were of an evening, and these people have two ironclad alibis."

"That's what I'm saying."

"Most people," Susan said. She looked at Hawk. "Except maybe for the man with the golden lance, here . . ."

"Black opal," Hawk said.

Susan nodded.

"Except for the man with the black-opal lance," she said. "Most people could go days at a time with no alibi except for whomever they live with."

"And," Hawk said. "If they both under suspicion . . ."

"The alibi is suspect," Susan said.

"Sorta," I said.

"You think they hired a third party?" Susan said.

"Yes."

"Both of them?" Susan said.

"I don't know," I said.

"Beth surely could not have escaped such a childhood unscathed," Susan said.

"Nobody do," Hawk said.

"She had somebody do Jackson," I said. "She'd get his money."

"She have somebody do Estelle," Susan said. "Beth would get Eisenhower."

"She don't get Jackson's money until somebody kills him," Hawk said. "How'd she pay."

I looked at him for a moment.

"Oh," Hawk said. "Yeah."

"What?" Susan said.

"She started out broke," I said. "How'd she pay her way this far?"

Susan was silent for a moment.

Then she said, "Oh. The, ah, barter system."

Our food came, and we ate some. Susan looked at Hawk.

"Well," she said.

Hawk nodded.

"Okay," he said. "You're right."

"Thank you," Susan said.

She looked at me.

"So if it were Beth, and if she were hiring somebody to kill her husband, and

Estelle, and taking it out in trade, who would she hire? Who does she know that she could hire?"

"Eisenhower's been in jail," I said. "Husband was on both sides of legitimate. She might know a lot of people, or she might know one who could broker the deal."

"She know Zel and Boo," Hawk said. "She know Tony Marcus."

"Ty-Bop?" I said.

"He don't freelance," Hawk said.

"Not even for love?" Susan said.

Hawk smiled at her.

"Ty-Bop don't know nothing 'bout love."

"Junior?" I said.

"Ain't a shooter," Hawk said.

"Probably knows how," I said.

"Maybe. You looking in that direction, I think you got to look at Tony. He tell Ty-Bop to shoot you. Ty-Bop will shoot you. He tell Junior to break your back. Junior will break your back. But gun work is Ty-Bop. And strong-arm is Junior. He don't ask one to do the other man specialty. And they don't do anything unless Tony tells them to. It's a matter of respect."

"You understand that?" Susan said to me.

"Yes," I said.

"But if Tony wanted Ty-Bop to shoot someone for love?"

"Ty-Bop do it," Hawk said.

"Does Tony know about love?" Susan said.

"Loves his daughter," Hawk said.

"So he's a possibility," Susan said.

"Yep," I said.

"But if you rule him out, you also rule out Ty-Bop and Junior," Susan said.

"Yep."

"How about this man Zel?" Susan said.

"Maybe," I said.

"Boo?"

"Hard to imagine Beth seducing any of these people," I said.

"Remember how far she's come, and how she got here," Susan said.

"You're saying she could?"

"If she needed to," Susan said.

"Could you?" I said.

"If I needed to," Susan said.

"Egad," I said.

Chapter

❖

57

TONY MARCUS CAME into my office wearing a double-breasted camel-hair coat and a Borsalino hat. Ty-Bop jangled in beside him and stood not quite motionless near the door.

"Arnold say you wanted to see me," Tony said.

He unbuttoned his coat, took his hat off, and put it on my desk, and sat down in front of me.

"I didn't know you still made house calls," I said.

"In the neighborhood," Tony said. "Going to have lunch with my daughter."

"Give her my best," I said.

"Sure," Tony said. "What you want?"

"You know Chet Jackson got whacked," I said.

Tony nodded.

"Couple days ago a woman named Estelle Gallagher got clipped with the same gun killed Jackson," I said.

Tony nodded.

"You keep track," I said.

"I do," Tony said.

"They're both connected with Gary Eisenhower," I said.

"Uh-huh."

Ty-Bop was studying the picture of Pearl that stood on top of a file cabinet just to the left of Susan's. I would have studied Susan had I been he, but Ty-Bop was mysterious.

"And Beth Jackson," I said.

"Uh-huh."

"You had any dealings with them since Jackson's office?" I said.

"You think one of them done the killings?" Tony said.

"They both have solid alibis," I said. "For both killings."

Tony smoothed his mustache with his left hand and nodded.

"Remarkable," he said.

"That's what I thought," I said.

"So you figured one or both contracted it out," Tony said.

"Maybe," I said.

"And you figure who they know might do it?"

"Yep."

"And you thought of me," Tony said.

"One possibility," I said.

Tony sat back in his chair and smoothed his mustache again. After a while he smiled.

"Yeah," he said. "We talked."

"How'd she get hold of you?"

"She called," Tony said. "Talk with Arnold."

"How'd she know where to call?" I said.

"Her husband had a number," he said.

"So the cops must have stopped by," I said.

"They did," Tony said. "I'm used to cops. Didn't tell them nothing. They didn't know nothing. They went away."

"What did Beth want?"

"She say she saw me in her husband's office that day and she thought I was very 'interesting.'" Tony grinned. "Say she want to see me."

"And?"

"And I say sure," Tony said.

"So you did," I said.

"Yep. Fucked her about sixteen times."

"Nice for you," I said.

Tony grinned.

"She enthusiastic," he said.

"But you didn't elope," I said.

"Nope, after we been fucking for a week or so, she say she need a favor."

"I'm shocked," I said.

"Yeah, I was surprised it took a week," Tony said. "Said she wanted somebody to ace her old man and could I help."

"And you said?"

"No."

"How'd she take that?"

"Not well. She say after all we meant to each other. And I say, 'I got nothing against your old man.' And she said, 'But don't you love me?' And I say no. And we go on like that. And finally I have Arnold take her out and drive her home."

"Give her a referral?"

"Hell, no," Tony said. "I put some people down, will again. But I did it 'cause it needed to be done. Not 'cause some broad bops me for a week."

"She have any other candidates?" I said.

"To pull the trigger for her?" Tony said. "There must have been one."

"But you have no idea?" I said.

"None."

"You have any sense that Eisenhower was involved?"

"Nope."

"Or that he wasn't?" I said.

"Nope."

I nodded. We were quiet. Ty-Bop had stopped looking at the picture of Pearl and was now, as best I could determine, looking at nothing I could identify. Tony picked up his hat, put it on, stood, and buttoned up his coat.

"You owe me," he said.

"But who keeps track," I said.

"Me," Tony said.

He nodded at Ty-Bop, who went out of the office first. Tony followed. They didn't close the door behind them. But that was okay. It created sort of a welcoming image. I was a friendly guy. Might be good for business.

Chapter

❖❖

58

VINNIE MORRIS WAS a middle-sized ordinary-looking guy who could shoot the tail off a buffalo nickel from fifty yards. We weren't exactly friends, but I'd known him since he walked behind Joe Broz, and while he wasn't all that much fun, he was good at what he did. He kept his word. And he didn't say much.

We were in my car, parked at a hydrant on Beacon Street beside the Public Garden, across the street from where Beth lived with Gary Eisenhower.

"Her name's Beth Jackson," I said. "We'll sit here and watch. If she comes out and gets in a car, we'll tail her. If she comes out and starts walking, you'll tail her."

"'Cause she knows you," Vinnie said.

"Yes."

Vinnie nodded.

"And that's it?" he said. "You want me to follow this broad around, tell you what I see?"

"Yep."

"I don't have to clip her?"

"No," I said.

"I don't like to clip no broad, I don't have to," Vinnie said.

"You won't have to," I said.

He looked at her picture.

"Nice head," he said.

"Yep."

"How long we gonna do this?" Vinnie said.

"Don't know."

"She takes a car and I just ride around with you," Vinnie said.

"Correct," I said.

"Okay," he said.

"You care why we're tailing her?" I said.

"Nope."

One of Vinnie's great charms was that he had no interest in any information he didn't need. We sat with Beth for several days. Mostly she walked. So mostly I stayed in the car and Vinnie hoofed it.

"She goes to Newbury Street," Vinnie said. "Meets different broads. They shop. They have lunch. Today it was in the café at Louis."

"Must be an adventure for you," I said.

"Yeah. I thought Louis was a men's store."

"All genders," I said.

"You buy stuff there?"

"Don't have my size," I said.

"Got my size," Vinnie said.

"See anything you like?" I said.

"Most of it looks kinda funny," Vinnie said.

"That's called stylish," I said.

"Not by me," Vinnie said.

"She spot you?"

Vinnie stared at me.

"Nobody spots me, I don't want to be spotted," Vinnie said.

"I don't know what I was thinking," I said.

We did that for most of a week, with Vinnie doing all the legwork and me twaddling in the car. On a white, dripping, above-freezing Friday in late February, I called it quits.

"You stick with her till I call you off," I said to Vinnie. "Or you can't stand it anymore. You don't need me. She's obviously a walking girl."

"I won't get sick of it," Vinnie said. "I like looking at her ass."

"Motivation is good," I said.

Vinnie got out of the car, and I drove home.

Chapter

❖

59

GARY EISENHOWER came to see me. I was in my office with my feet up, listening to some Anita O'Day songs on my office computer and thinking lightly.

"Who's the broad singing," Gary said when he came in.

"Anita O'Day," I said.

"I need to talk," he said.

I turned Anita off and swiveled my full attention to him.

"Go," I said.

He sat in one of my client chairs.

"I . . ."

He shifted a little and crossed one leg over the other.

"I . . . I feel really bad," he said. "About Estelle."

I nodded.

"And I . . . I . . . I got no one else to talk to about it," he said.

"Happy to be the one," I said.

"I mean, I been with Estelle for, like, ten years," Gary said.

"Long time," I said.

"I . . . I cared about her."

"Through all the philandering" I said.

"Sure, I told you. She liked it, too. We were in that together."

I nodded.

"For crissake, who would want to kill Estelle," Gary said.

I shook my head. I wanted to go where he wanted to. I suspected he was circling it. He shifted in his chair and crossed his legs in the other direction. He tapped out a little drumbeat on his thighs for a moment.

"The thing is," he said. "The thing that kills me is . . . did I do something to cause this?"

I looked interested.

"I mean," he said, "did I, like . . . did I bring her into contact with someone who would kill her?"

I waited. He didn't say anything else. I waited some more. He interlocked his fingers and worked his hands back and forth. Clarice Richardson had been wrong, I thought. Gary was not devoid of something like a moral or ethical sense. Whatever it quite was, it was nagging at him now. He looked at me. The sense had apparently taken him as far as it was going to. Probably wasn't a very robust sense to begin with.

"I mean, why would someone kill her?" he said again.

"Money," I said. "Love and the stuff that goes with it."

"What stuff?" he said.

"Passion, jealousy, and hate," I said.

"Estelle didn't like Beth living with us," Gary said.

I nodded.

"I mean, she did at first," he said. "You know, she liked the money, and the truth of it is, she liked the three-way for a while."

"And you said you liked it okay," I said.

He smiled briefly, and for a moment the old Gary shone through.

"Hell," he said. "I like everything."

"Beth like the three-way?" I said.

"She never said she didn't," he said.

"So why didn't Estelle like Beth living there?" I said.

"I don't know," Gary said. "I mean, women are a pretty weird species."

"One of the two weirdest," I said.

Gary looked blank. Then he kind of shook it off.

"Anyway, Estelle started saying stuff like Beth was getting too bossy, and how we couldn't get any privacy."

"She say that to Beth?"

"I don't think so," Gary said. "She said it to me quite a bit toward the end. But I never heard her talk to Beth about it."

"You say anything to Beth?" I said.

"Me? No. I learned a long time ago to stay out of a catfight."

"You think Beth might have killed Estelle so she could have you to herself?" I said.

"We was at the big Community Servings

event, at the Langham," Gary said. "Cops told us when she died. Beth couldn'ta done it."

He said it too fast. Like he'd rehearsed it.

"The Hotel Langham affair your idea?" I said.

"Me? No. Beth wanted to go. Said she knew a lotta people went to it. Said she wanted them to see her boyfriend."

"You say anything about being Estelle's boyfriend?"

"Hell," Gary said. And there was no bravado in his voice. "I'm everybody's boyfriend."

"And Estelle's dead," I said.

Gary didn't speak. He nodded his head slowly, and as he did, tears began to well in his eyes.

NOT GOOD FOR
ME — NOT
WELL WRITTEN

STORY NOT GOOD

Chapter

❖❖

60

HAWK CAME TO MY PLACE to babysit Pearl, and Susan went with me to New York for fun. We stopped for a tongue sandwich at Rein's deli on the way down. I made several amusing tongue remarks while we ate, which Susan said were disgusting. That night we stayed uptown at The Carlyle, had dinner at Café Boulud, and went to bed before midnight.

I was prepared for several hours of wild abandon when I got into bed. But by the time Susan got through with her nocturnal ablutions, I had nodded off. I woke up in the morning with Susan's head on my chest.

I shifted a little so I could look at her. She opened her eyes and we looked at each other. She moved a little so we were facing.

"You've always been an early riser," Susan said.

"Is that a double entendre?" I said.

"I think so," Susan said.

"Shall we take advantage of it?" I said.

"Right after we shower and brush our teeth," Susan said.

"By then it may be too late," I said.

She smiled. And got out of bed.

"Not you and me, big boy," she said. "For us it's never too late."

"How come you sleep in sweatpants and a T-shirt?" I said.

She smiled again.

"So that when I take them off," she said, "the contrast makes me look really good."

"It works," I said.

"Yes," she said, and went into the bathroom and turned on the shower.

A half-hour later we were both back in bed, clean of body and mouth. When Susan made love she went deep inside someplace. She didn't withdraw. It was just the intensity of her focus that rendered everything except the lovemaking irrelevant. I liked to look at her then, her eyes closed, her face perfectly still, calm in contrast to what we both were feeling and doing. The event was busy enough so I couldn't look for very long, but when we were done and I was looking down at her, after a time she opened her eyes and looked at me and I could see her slowly refocusing, swimming back to the surface from wherever she had been. It was always a moment like no other.

"You lookin' at me," Susan said in a surprisingly good De Niro impression.

"Sex is a complicated thing," I said.

Susan widened her eyes.

"Wow," she said.

"It enhances love," I said. "But not as much as love enhances it."

"You've noticed that," Susan said.

"I have."

"And you may be particularly aware of that interplay these days," Susan said. "Because of this business with Gary Eisenhower and the women."

"I would guess," I said.

Susan and I stayed in eye lock, another moment, then. She smiled.

"Perhaps," she said, "if you would get

your two-hundred-something pounds off of my body, I could breathe and we could discuss it over breakfast."

"You were breathing good a little while ago," I said.

"Gasping," Susan said.

"In awe?" I said.

"For breath," she said.

I eased off her and lay on my back beside her, and she put her head on my shoulder.

"I mean, the old jokes are all true. The worst sex I ever had was very good. But I have never had a sexual experience to compare to making love with you."

"Jewesses are hot," Susan said.

"You are beautiful, and in shape, and skillful, and enthusiastic. But I have been with many other women who fit that description close enough. But nothing to compare with you."

Susan turned her head so that she could look at me.

"There's a saying I read someplace, that appetite is the best sauce," she said.

"Meaning it's not just what you are, it's what I feel you are," I said.

"I would guess," she said, "in truth, that it is finally about what and who we are."

I nodded.

"It's what Gary Eisenhower and his women don't understand, and probably never will," I said.

"It is probably life's essence," Susan said.

I nodded.

"Maybe children, too," I said.

"Maybe," Susan said. "But we're not going to have any."

"This'll have to do," I said.

"It does very well," she said.

She kissed me. I kissed her back.

"I'm thinking pancakes for breakfast," she said.

Chapter

61

WE HAD PANCAKES for breakfast and walked down through Central park to Bergdorf and Barneys, where Susan shopped and I trailed along to watch her hold stuff up, and admire her and, occasionally, some of the other female shoppers. In the next couple of days, we strolled through the little zoo in Central Park. We had dinner at the Four Seasons and walked through Rockefeller Center and Grand Central Station, which I always liked to do in New York. We experienced life's essence several times before we went home.

Life's essence never disappoints.

It was a Wednesday morning when I

got back to my office. There was a call on my answering machine from Vinnie.

"Call me," he said. "I might have something."

I called him on his cell phone.

"Where are you?" I said.

"In the Public Garden," he said, "watching her house."

"What's up?" I said.

"Nothing at the moment, but Monday she had a, like, a incident with a guy."

"Tell me," I said.

"Guy's waiting outside her house when she comes back from her health club. I'm trailing along behind, looking at her ass, and he, like, stops her as she starts up her steps. Puts his hand on her arm. She slaps it away. He says something. She says something. He puts his hand on her arm again. She shoves him away and runs up the steps into her house. He stands down at the foot of the stairs for a long time and looks at her front door. I'm up the street thinking if he tries to go in after her do I shoot him. But he didn't. After a while he walked away."

"It wasn't a friendly exchange," I said.

"No."

"You recognize the guy?"

"No, but he wasn't her type, that's for sure."

"What'd he look like?" I said.

"Big guy, 'bout your size, but, you know, he was walking on his heels."

"Like punch-drunk?" I said. "Like a punch-drunk ex-fighter?"

"Be my guess," Vinnie said. "Looked like a pug, nose was flat, and, you know, thick around the eyes."

"Anybody with him?" I said.

"Nope."

"Where'd he go after she went in and he stared at the door?"

"Walked down Arlington Street. I figured he was heading for the subway."

"You didn't follow him?"

"Nope. You just tole me to watch the broad."

"I did," I said. "Anything else happen?"

"Nope. She stayed in all the rest of the day."

"No sign that she called the cops?" I said.

"None showed up," he said. "This guy shows up again, you want me to shoot him or anything?"

"Only if you have to," I said.

"Okay," Vinnie said.

"I may stop around later and visit Beth," I said.

"Okay," Vinnie said.

"Don't shoot me."

"Okay," Vinnie said.

He sounded disappointed.

Chapter

················◆◆················

62

WHEN BETH JACKSON came out of Pinnacle Fitness and into the lobby, I was waiting for her.

"Buy you coffee," I said.

She looked at me as if I was something she stepped in.

"I don't want coffee," she said.

"I'll buy you whatever you want," I said.

"I don't want anything," she said.

"Well, here's the thing," I said. "I'm going to keep annoying you until you talk with me for a little while, so why not get it over with now."

"If you continue to annoy me," she said, "I shall call the police."

"Sure," I said. "In the meantime, lemme buy you some coffee and talk with you about Boo."

She stared at me for a moment, then sighed.

"Very well," she said, and stalked ahead of me to the snack bar.

I knew Boo would get her, and if it didn't, it would mean whoever Vinnie saw wasn't Boo. If it was Boo, she would have to talk to me enough to find out what I knew. We ordered coffee.

"What about this Boo person, or whatever Boo is?" she said.

"Boo is the slugger used to work for your husband," I said. "He and a guy named Zel."

The coffee arrived. I added some sugar and took a swallow.

"Oh," she said, "Boo. I hadn't thought of Boo since Chet died."

"Until Monday," I said.

"Monday?"

"Boo stopped you in front of your house. You and he argued. You shoved him and went in. He stayed outside for a while and looked at your door."

She didn't say anything. She looked at me silently for a long time. I let her look. I was interested in what she'd come up with.

Finally she said, "Are you spying on me?"

"Yuh," I said.

"Why?"

"What did Boo want?" I said.

"Boo," she said. "So that's who that was."

"You didn't recognize him," I said.

"No. I mean, I thought he looked familiar, but . . . no."

"And what did he want?" I said.

"Oh, God," she said. "I have no idea. I thought he was some kind of stumblebum, you know? I just wanted him to leave me alone."

I nodded.

"And I object to you lurking around spying."

"Noted," I said.

"Why are you doing that?"

"Got nothing else to do," I said.

"Do you think I'm doing something bad?"

"Are you?" I said.

"Gary and I are just trying to live our lives," she said, "in the midst of terrible tragedy."

"Boo want money?" I said.

"No . . . I don't know. . . . I just wanted to get away from him," she said.

"What's the first thing he said to you?"

Her face got sort of squeezed up. Her cheeks reddened a little.

"I won't talk about this anymore," she said. "I've done nothing wrong, and I won't let you question me as if I have."

She stood up abruptly and walked to the elevator. I watched her go.

Spenser, the grand inquisitor.

Chapter

❖

63

ONE OF SPENSER'S RULES for criminal investigation is that most things have two ends. I'd gotten nothing much from Beth's end, so I decided to try the other end, and went out to JP to visit Boo.

Zel was cooking sausage and peppers when I got there, and I sat at the kitchen table and drank a beer he gave me while he cooked.

"Boo ain't here," Zel said.

"Where is he?" I said.

"Out," Zel said.

"What's he doing while he's out?" I said.

"Got me," Zel said.

He moved the peppers and sausage around with a spatula.

"Low heat," Zel said. "Cook it slow. That's the secret."

"He go out much alone?"

Zel looked at me.

"Boo's forty-two years old," he said. "Course he goes out alone."

I nodded.

"You and he doing any business with Beth Jackson?" I said.

"Beth? Chet's wife? No, thank you," Zel said.

"Trouble?" I said.

"With a capital T," Zel said. "And that rhymes with B, and that stands for bitch."

"You don't like Beth," I said.

"Good call," Zel said.

"I'm a trained detective," I said.

"No," Zel said. "I don't like her."

"Because?"

"Because I kind of liked Chet."

"And she cheated on him," I said.

"She didn't give him no respect," Zel said.

I nodded.

"Boo like her?" I said.

Zel looked at me sharply.

"Why?"

"He had a confrontation with her Monday," I said. "Outside her house."

"Shit!" Zel said.

He poured some sherry wine over the sausage and peppers and watched it boil up briefly and then start to cook away. He lowered the heat to simmer, then turned from the stove and went to the refrigerator and got a bottle of beer for himself and another one for me. He put mine on the table in front of me and went and leaned on the counter near the stove. He drank some of his beer and looked at me.

"Boo ain't right," he said. "We both know that."

I nodded.

"But like I said, he's forty-two years old. I try to look out for him, but . . . I can't treat him like a little kid."

"He'd know it?" I said.

"It would be disrespectful," Zel said.

I nodded.

"But . . ."

Zel drank some more beer and checked his cooking.

"But Boo can't do time," Zel said. "He's okay if I'm with him, but if I ain't, he can't stand close places."

"Claustrophobic?" I said.

"Yeah, that's what he is, claustrophobic. 'Less I'm with him, he can't ride an elevator. Can't go in the subway if it's crowded. Has to leave the window open in his room a crack, no matter how cold it is."

"But he's all right if he's with you?"

"Yeah."

"Why are you worried about him doing time?" I said.

Zel checked his cooking again and shut off the heat under his pan.

"You ain't here to sell him magazine subscriptions," Zel said.

"You know why he would be having an argument with Beth Jackson?" I said.

Zel got another beer from the refrigerator. He held one toward me. I shook my head.

"Another thing," Zel said, "about Boo. He gotta be a tough guy. It's all he ever had, being a tough guy."

"And he's not so good at that," I said.

"Not against somebody like you," Zel said. "But for Boo, it almost don't matter if he wins. He gotta fight, you know? He wins, or he shows he can take it. Either way, he gotta be a tough guy."

Zel drank some beer.

"All he got," Zel said. "He does time, he'll be scared, and he can't stand to be scared, so he'll be a tough guy and he'll get hurt bad. Don't matter how tough you are. Inside, they can break you."

"You've been inside," I said.

"Uh-huh."

"And Boo," I said.

"What's made him so . . . odd," Zel said. "I mean, he started out with a lot of problems, and he was always kinda slow. But time in made all of it much worse."

"You know what he's doing with Beth Jackson?" I said.

"No."

"You know who killed Chet Jackson and Estelle Gallagher?"

"No."

"You think Boo was involved?" I said.

"Boo's mostly a slugger," Zel said.

"He had a gun when I was here last," I said.

Zel nodded.

"So you think he was involved?" I said.

"No."

"If he was, I'm gonna find it out," I said.

"He wasn't," Zel said. "I'd know."

"I think he was," I said.

Zel nodded.

"He can't do no time," Zel said.

Chapter

64

VINNIE CALLED ME at home from his cell phone. It was nine-eleven at night. I was watching the Celtics game.

"You might want to know this," he said.

"I might," I said.

I muted the sound on the television.

"Been watching Beth's ass all day. Followed her home from the club, 'bout five-fifteen, watched her go in. 'Bout six o'clock the boyfriend comes home. I watch him go in. By seven I figure they're in for the night, so I call it a day. I walk down Arlington to the Ritz, Taj, whatever the fuck it is now, and go in to take a leak. Then I'm in

there, I figure I'll go in the bar, have a couple pops, think about Beth's ass, which I
would now recognize at three miles in the
dark. So I'm in there for maybe an hour or
so, and I have a few, and then I go out and
head down Arlington to get my car. I know
a guy works the door at The Park Plaza,
and he's holding my car for me."

"Uh-huh," I said.

The Celtics were up four on the Wiz-
ards late in the first half.

"And I see the pug," Vinnie said.

I shut off the television.

"Boo?" I said.

"Same guy had the argument with Beth
a while back," Vinnie said. "He's walking
along Arlington same direction I am, like
he could have been down at Beth's place.
He's on the other side of the street. So I
slow down and sort of let him get ahead of
me and I see what he does. He crosses
over in front of me at Boylston and goes
into the subway. So I chuck along after him
and go down, too."

"Was it crowded?" I said.

"Naw," Vinnie said. "Place was empty.
So he goes through the turnstile and waits
on the outbound platform, and I don't see

any reason to waste two bucks, so I go back upstairs and get my car. On my way home I swung by Beth's building, but everything looked, you know, copacetic, so I kept going."

"Thank you, Vinnie," I said.

We hung up.

I dialed Gary Eisenhower's number. After four rings the answering machine picked up.

"Hi, it's Beth. Neither Gary nor I can come to the phone right now, but your call is important to us, so please do leave a message, and we'll get back to you as quick as we can."

When the beep sounded I yelled a couple of times that it was Spenser and pick up the phone. But nothing happened, so I hung up and got dressed and took a gun and hoofed it down to the apartment that Beth now shared with Gary, which was only a couple of blocks from my place.

The front door was locked. I rang Gary's bell; nothing happened. I rang a few other bells. One of the tenants answered. It was a woman.

"Hi," I said. "It's Gary from the first floor.

I seem to have the wrong front-door key. Could you buzz me in."

"Call the super," she said, and broke the connection.

Neighborly.

I found the superintendent's number and rang the bell. After two rings he answered, sounding foggy.

"Yeah?"

"Police," I said. "I need you to come open a couple doors for me."

"Police?" he said.

"You heard me, now run your ass up here."

"Yeah, yeah, sure, officer, gimme a minute."

It took more than a minute, but it was only two or three before he appeared in the entryway and opened the door.

"You ain't wearing a uniform," he said.

"No shit," I said.

"You got a badge or something?"

I looked at him hard.

I said, "Ain't I seen a mug shot of you, pal?"

"Me? I never done nothing."

"That's your story. Open up apartment

one-A pretty goddamned hubba hubba, or I'll run your ass down to the station for a look-see."

"One-A, yeah, sure," he said, and took out his key ring. "No need to get all worked up."

"Move it," I said. "Or I'll work you up, you unnerstand that?"

"Yes, sir, sure thing."

He went to Gary's door and unlocked it. I went in. The super came in behind me a step.

"Jesus," he said. "Jesus Christ."

"Call nine-one-one," I said. "Cops and an ambulance."

"But you're a . . ."

"Call it," I said.

Chapter

65

BETH WAS DEAD, I knew that the minute I saw her. Her face was bruised, there was dried blood, and her neck was turned at an odd angle. Gary was unconscious but not dead. He had a big purple bruise on the side of his face at the hairline. But he was breathing pretty steadily, and his pulse wasn't bad.

The super, having called 911, stood in the doorway, as if he didn't dare enter and he didn't dare leave. It was maybe three minutes before two uniforms came into the room.

"He says he's a cop," he told one of the cops.

"That right?" the cop said to me.

He was a thick-necked guy with a red face, and he was showing signs of sitting down too much. His partner was a younger guy, black, with sort of economical movements. The black cop squatted on the floor beside me and felt the pulse in Gary's neck. He nodded to himself and moved over to Beth.

"Right," I said.

"Show me something," the cop said.

"I'm private," I said.

"Impersonating an officer?" the red-faced cop said.

"Exactly," I said.

Squatting by Beth, the cop felt for her pulse and didn't find it. He stood.

"Charlie," he said. "We seem to have a murder here. Maybe you could postpone the impersonating-an-officer investigation till we solve this."

The red-faced cop looked at him a moment, and at me.

"They dead?" he said.

"She is. The guy seems like he'll make it," the black cop said.

The red-faced cop walked past me and looked at Beth.

"Shame," he said.

Two paramedics came in.

"Broad's dead," the white cop said. "Work on the other guy?"

One of the paramedics was a stocky blonde woman.

"Lemme check," she said, and crouched beside Beth. The male paramedic started on Gary.

Charlie walked out into the foyer and began to talk on his radio. The black cop came to me.

"My name's Harper," he said. "What's yours?"

I told him.

"ID?"

I took out my license and my carry permit. The black cop looked at it.

"You carrying a weapon now?" he said.

"Yes," I said.

"I'll hold on to it for a while," he said.

I opened my coat so he could see the gun.

"You can take it out," Harper said. "Just go easy."

I took the gun off my hip and handed it

to him. It was a short-barreled .38 revolver. Reliable. Easy to carry.

"You hit anything with this?" Harper said.

"Ten, fifteen feet," I said.

"All you need," Harper said, and put the gun in a pocket of his uniform jacket.

Belson came into the apartment with some crime-scene people and two homicide detectives.

"This guy," Charlie said, and looked at his notebook, "Spenser. He was impersonating a police officer."

Belson glanced at him.

"We all thought that," Belson said, "when he *was* a cop."

"Was carrying," Harper said. "With a permit. I got the piece."

"Give it back to him," Belson said.

Harper shrugged and handed me my gun.

Belson looked at the super.

"Who's this?" he said.

"I'm the superintendent. He told me he was a cop."

Belson nodded.

"Fucking crime wave in here," he said.

He nodded at one of the detectives.

"Get a statement from the super," he said.

Then he looked at the paramedics.
"Woman dead?"

"Yes, Sergeant," the woman said. "Appears to be blunt-instrument trauma."

"Guy?"

"He's way out," she said. "But vital signs are steady. He should come around."

"When?"

The woman shrugged.

"When he does," she said.

"You taking him to City?"

"We call that Boston Medical Center now," she said.

"You taking him there?" Belson said.

"Yes."

Belson turned to Harper and his partner.

"You two go with him. Make sure nobody tries to finish the job. When he wakes up, call me."

"What about her?" the paramedic said.

"Coroner will take her away. Right now she's evidence."

The medics put Gary on a stretcher, stabilized him, and took him to the ambulance. Charlie and Harper went with them. Belson turned to me.

"Impersonating a police officer," Belson said.

342 ROBERT B. PARKER

He was looking at the room as he talked to me. He always did that at a crime scene, and when he left, I knew he would have seen everything in the room, and he'd remember it.

"Mea culpa," I said.

"How many times you done that now," Belson said, "since I knew you?"

"Sixty-three times, I think."

Belson nodded, still slowly absorbing the room.

"Tell me what you know," he said.

Chapter

66

I DON'T KNOW QUITE why I left Boo out of it, but I did.

When Gary woke up he'd tell them what happened, and they'd come for Boo. I wanted a little time to get there first. I didn't quite know why I wanted to get there first. I left Vinnie out, too—professional courtesy. I said that I'd been watching her place and seen somebody suspicious-looking come out of the building. So I'd called on my cell and got no answer. The rest of it I told as it happened.

I don't think Frank bought it all, he came at it from a few different directions, but my story didn't change and Frank let it go. He knew I hadn't done it. And he knew that sooner or later, he and I were working the same side of the street.

Mostly.

I got to JP a little before midnight. There was a light on in the window of the second-floor apartment that Boo shared with Zel. I rang the bell. After a minute Zel came to the door, and looked out and saw it was me, and opened the door.

"Trouble?" he said.

"Where's Boo?" I said.

"He ain't here, ain't been home all day."

"We need to talk," I said.

Zel nodded and stepped aside. He closed the door behind me and preceded me up the dim stairway. He had a gun in his right hip pocket.

In the kitchen, we sat on opposite sides of the table, under a single naked bulb.

"What?" Zel said.

I looked around the apartment. It wasn't much. Two bedrooms, a bath, and a kitchen. The doors to all the other rooms were open to the kitchen. There was no sign of Boo.

"Boo killed Beth Jackson tonight," I said. "Beat her to death."

Zel didn't move. He didn't change his expression.

"Cops know she's dead, but they don't know yet that it was Boo."

Zel nodded slightly.

"But you do," he said.

"Yeah," I said. "But they'll know soon enough. Boo left an eyewitness alive."

Zel shook his head sadly.

"Poor dumb bastard," Zel said.

"Gary Eisenhower," I said. "He was unconscious when we found him, but when he wakes up, he'll pretty sure be mentioning Boo's name."

Zel nodded.

"So why are you here," Zel said.

I paused. The room wasn't much, but it was neat. No dirty dishes, no crumbs on the table. The refrigerator was old and made a lot of noise. Otherwise, there was no sound anywhere, and no sense that there was anyone alive in the building but me and Zel under the one-hundred-watt bulb.

"I don't know," I said. "I just figured I oughta talk with you before the cops came to get him."

"Boo won't want to go," Zel said.

"They'll come in large numbers," I said.

"Yeah," Zel said. "They do that."

He got up and got two bottles of beer from the refrigerator and gave me one and sat down again.

"You know why he killed her?" I said.

"I got an idea," Zel said.

I nodded.

"Here's my theory," I said. "See what you think."

Zel nodded.

"I figure she came on to him," I said.

Zel turned the beer bottle on the table-top and didn't say anything.

"I figure she came on to him so she could get him to kill her husband," I said.

"Why'd she want him dead?" Zel said, watching the bottle as he turned it slowly, as if turning it just right was as important as anything he was going to do this day.

"So she'd get his money," I said. "And be with Gary Eisenhower."

"And why Boo?" Zel said.

"She didn't know anybody else," I said. "She tried Tony Marcus, didn't work."

"She thought it would?" Zel said.

"She had a lot of faith in sex," I said.

Zel nodded and stopped twirling his bottle long enough to drink some beer.

"So Boo goes for it and pops Jackson," I said. "And she gets his dough and moves in with Gary and Estelle."

"Three of them," Zel said.

"Yep. I guess Estelle kind of liked the idea."

Zel shrugged.

"But it didn't work," I said. "Pretty soon Beth wants all of Gary, and Estelle don't like it."

Zel was twirling his bottle again. He hadn't drunk much of his beer. I hadn't drunk any of mine.

"So," I said. "Beth calls in Boo, and with the same gun he used on Jackson, he pops Estelle for her."

"Dumb," Zel said, and shook his head sadly. "Dumb."

"So there's Beth, thanks to Boo, right where she wants to be. Money, Gary"—I raised my hands—"what could be better."

Zel drank some beer.

"But . . ."

Zel nodded.

"But Boo thinks that he's done her these

two huge favors," I said. "So she's supposed to love him."

"Boo never been with any women but
whores, I think," Zel said.

"And Beth thinks that since she bopped
him several times, she's done him several
huge favors," I said, "and wants no more
to do with him."

Zel nodded. His beer was gone. He got
up and got another one from the refrigerator, looked at my bottle, saw that it was
full, and sat down.

"They had a confrontation a week or so
ago," I said. "He tries to talk with her, she
shoves him and runs inside. Middle of the
day, Boo stands for a while and walks away."

"You was following him?" Zel said.

I shook my head.

"Had a guy on her," I said.

"So you been thinking about her for a
while," Zel said.

"Yes."

"Was the guy watching tonight?" Zel
said.

"Was through for the night," I said. "And
having a drink in the Taj bar. When he comes
out, he sees Boo heading away from Gary's
apartment and calls me."

"And you figure Boo went over there, kicked in the door, decked her boyfriend, and beat her to death?"

"Something like that," I said.

"Why tonight?" Zel said.

I shrugged.

"Love unrequited," I said. "The pressure built. He drink?"

"Some," Zel said. "I tried to keep him from drinking much, but he's hard to control."

"Bad when he's drunk?"

"Yes."

"Will he come back here?" I said.

"Sooner or later," Zel said. "Except I can shoot, I ain't much, and Boo's less. But we been together a long time."

"He's killed three people," I said.

"He can't do no time," Zel said. "I tole you that."

"I can't let him walk around loose," I said.

Zel looked at his beer bottle for a moment.

"I know," he said.

We sat for a moment. Then I stood.

"Thanks for the beer," I said.

And I left.

Chapter

❖

67

Boo came home about two-thirty this afternoon," I said to Susan.

"You have someone watching?" she said.

"Vinnie," I said. "And Hawk. Vinnie's there now."

We were in Susan's living room, upstairs from her office. Susan usually had a glass of wine after her last patient, and when I could, I liked to join her. In honor of that, Susan had stocked some Sam Adams Winter Ale, which I was especially fond of, and I was having some while she sipped her wine.

"Did Gary wake up yet?" Susan said.

"He's coming around, Belson says. But he's still foggy."

"What are you going to do about Boo?" Susan said.

"I don't know," I said.

"You don't want to turn him in," Susan said.

"He's not right in the head," I said.

"And Beth exploited him," Susan said.

"Yes."

"You can't let him go," Susan said.

"I know."

"So," Susan said. "Basically you're stalling."

"I am," I said.

"What do you hope will happen?" Susan said.

"Mostly I'm hoping you'll stop asking me about it," I said.

Susan looked at me silently for a moment.

Then she said, "Wow. This is really bothering you."

"Yes."

"And you don't want to talk about it," she said.

"No," I said.

Susan stood and went to the kitchen.

She got a second bottle of Winter Ale from the refrigerator, popped the cap, brought the bottle back, and set it on the coffee table in front of me. Then she kissed me on the top of the head and went back and sat down on the couch. Pearl, who was sleeping at the other end of the couch with her head hanging over the arm, raised her head up for a minute and looked at Susan, saw that there was no food forthcoming, and put her head back down.

"We won't talk about Boo," Susan said.

"Good," I said.

"But we could talk about Beth and Estelle and Gary," Susan said. "And their circle."

"Sure," I said.

"In one way or another, they all earned what happened to them," Susan said.

"None of them earned getting murdered," I said.

"Does anyone?" Susan said.

"Sometimes, maybe," I said. "I don't want to generalize."

"No," Susan said. "You almost never do. But at the heart of all this is their own behavior."

"Especially Gary," I said.

"Yes."

"Boys just want to have fun," I said.

"This boy exploited the pathologies of women," Susan said.

"And it caught up with him," I said.

"Pathologies are pathologies," Susan said. "They don't go away when you're through using them."

I nodded.

"Thing is," I said. "He probably had no intention that any of this would happen."

"No," Susan said. "Probably not. He's just careless. And he went around spreading his careless good times."

"And making money at it."

"Yes, that makes it a little worse," Susan said. "But I suspect that was just a nice side effect."

"Like a guy likes to go to the track," I said. "He likes to hang around the paddock when the horses come out. He likes to look at them. Likes to handicap. Likes to watch them run. And if he happens to win some money, even better."

"But if he doesn't win, he still goes to the track," Susan said.

"Yes."

"Fun-loving Gary," Susan said.

"And three people are dead," I said.

Susan smiled sadly.

"And what do you think of your blue-eyed boy now?" she said.

Chapter

......................................◆◆◆......................................

68

I SPENT THE NIGHT with Susan, which improved my frame of mind, as it always did.
She had early clients, so I was in my office
at eight thirty-five the next morning. Neither Hawk nor Vinnie had seen any sign of
Boo since he'd arrived home yesterday.

I was pouring my second cup of coffee
when Quirk came into my office and shut
the door behind him.

"Coffee?" I said.

"Yeah," Quirk said.

He took off his overcoat and folded it
carefully over the arm of Pearl's sofa, then
came and sat in a chair opposite my desk.

356 ROBERT B. PARKER

I gave him a cup of coffee and went around my desk and sat down.

"Gary Eisenhower's awake," Quirk said.

"Uh-huh."

"He don't remember a thing," Quirk said.

"Who hit him?" I said. "Nothing?"

"He remembers the front doorbell," Quirk said, "and opening the door."

"That's it?"

"So far," Quirk said. "Doctors tell me it may come, may not. I guess he took a couple good shots to the head and probably hit the back of his head when he fell."

"Repeated blunt-force trauma," I said.

"You been watching those doctor shows," Quirk said.

"How else I gonna learn?" I said.

"Best any of us can figure," Quirk said. "It was a fist."

"Big fist," I said.

"And somebody who knew how to punch," Quirk said.

"How about Beth?" I said, just to be saying something.

"Same with the broad," Quirk said. "Apparently, she was punched to death."

"So you're looking for a guy knows how to punch," I said.

"You know how to punch," Quirk said.

"I do," I said. "On the other hand, so do you."

Quirk smiled slightly.

"And it wasn't either of us," Quirk said.

"No," I said.

"I figure," Quirk said, "guy didn't set out to kill anyone. Even guys who can fight don't normally set out to kill somebody with their hands."

"You figure he'd have brought a weapon," I said.

"I do."

I nodded.

"Confident guy," Quirk said. "Kicks in the door on some broad's apartment where she lives with her boyfriend, and apparently doesn't even bring a weapon."

"Or too mad to think," I said.

"What would he be so mad about?"

"What are they usually so mad about?" I said.

"Crime of passion?" Quirk said.

"Lot of that going around," I said.

Quirk nodded. He finished his coffee and got up and poured himself some more. He added sugar and condensed milk and took it back to his chair.

"Frank thinks you're not giving us everything," Quirk said.

"How unkind of Frank," I said.

"Yeah, sure," Quirk said. "You giving us everything?"

I drank some coffee and leaned back a little in my chair.

"You and me?" I said.

"You see anybody else here?" Quirk said.

"No," I said. "I'm not giving you everything."

"You know who killed her, don't you," Quirk said.

"Yes," I said.

"And you're holding that back why?" Quirk said.

"I'm not quite sure. But I won't tell you yet."

"I'm not sure the law lets you decide that," Quirk said.

"Sure," I said. "I know. You can bust me for interfering with an investigation, or some such, and take me downtown, and Rita Fiore will be along in an hour or so to get me out."

"You might be a little worse for wear," Quirk said.

"I might," I said.

"But we wouldn't have learned any-thing," Quirk said.

"True."

"When you gonna tell me?" Quirk said.

"Soon," I said.

Quirk nodded slowly.

"I known you a long time," Quirk said. "You are what you are."

I shrugged.

"Killer gets away," Quirk said, "because you stalled me, I'll come down on you as hard as I can."

"Which is quite hard," I said.

Quirk nodded.

"It is," he said, and stood and left my office.

I swiveled my chair around and looked out my window. It was bright and cold. Baseball was little more than a month away. The windows in the high-rises across the street were blank today, reflecting the morn-ing light so that I couldn't see through any of them.

It seemed simple enough. Boo had killed three people. I knew it. I tell Quirk. Quirk busts him. Case closed.

So why not?

I don't know.

I sat and looked up at the blue sky and across at the blank windows for a long time. A woman I'd once cared about had worked in an advertising agency over there. Sometimes, when the sun came at them from a different angle, I could see through the windows across the street and watch her moving about her office. Agency was gone now. Maybe the whole building was gone, replaced by a new one. It was hard to remember.

Chapter

❖❖

69

I WAS STILL LOOKING at the blank windows and the hard, blue sky an hour later when the door opened behind me. I turned my chair. It was Zel. He closed the door behind him and came to my desk and stood. He didn't take his coat off.

"I'm leaving town," he said.

I nodded.

"Where you going?" I said.

"Away," Zel said.

"Happening place," I said.

He stood. I sat. Neither of us spoke. Finally he said, "Boo's dead."

I nodded.

"You do it?" I said.

"Yeah," Zel said.

"Means he won't have to do time," I said.

"He come home in the afternoon, sort of all jeeped up, you know. Talking real fast, not sitting down, and I told him you'd been there, and what you said about him and Beth. And he's listening, but he's sort of walking around like before a fight, you know? He's moving his shoulders, bouncing a little on his toes. Moving his fists like he's warming up."

I nodded.

"So I ask him, did he do it?" Zel said.

"And he stops everything, stands there like a statue, and looks at me. 'Yeah,' he tells me. 'I done her.'"

I took in some air.

"And I ask him, 'Why?'" Zel said. "And he tells me she's a lying bitch and didn't mean nothing she told him, and she just said what she said and done what she done so he'd do stuff for her."

"Like kill her husband and Estelle," I said.

Zel nodded.

"He was right," I said.

"Yeah," Zel said. "So I say to him he's